BEACHFRONT EMBRACE

SOLOMONS ISLAND BOOK THREE

MICHELE GILCREST

CHAPTER 1

Clara opened the front door to the sight of her sister, Agnes, standing on the other side of the threshold. She had a duffle bag on the ground beside her and wore sunglasses that appeared to cover up a black and blue shiner on her face. She hadn't seen her since the day she left New York. It was the same day she left Keith, her ex-husband, and the day she left the weight of a tumultuous marriage behind her. Now, here she was, almost ten years later, standing at the doorstep of her Beachfront mansion.

"Agnes?"

"Hi, Clara."

She stood with a stoic expression before picking up her designer bag.

"Mind if I come in?"

Holly, Clara's dog, danced around Agnes' feet, rapidly wagging her tail and barking.

Feeling surprised, Clara continued to stare.

"Wasn't expecting to see you here. How did you find me?" Clara asked.

"It's easy finding people nowadays. Your information was just a click away. I think they call it the World Wide Web. Do you mind?" she asked, walking closer to enter in.

Clara held her arm out, motioning for her to walk in.

This has to be a bad dream. Either that or someone is playing a sick prank on me.

"Make yourself at home," she said sarcastically.

Agnes checked out her surroundings while making her way to the back and pulling up a seat in the kitchen, as if she were in familiar territory.

"I always imagined we'd cross paths again. But, I have to say... you definitely caught me off guard with this one, Agnes. I was minutes away from leaving the house. Do you mind explaining what's going on?"

Clara's voice was low as she tried to maintain her cool and make sense of things.

"I will, but you might want to grab a drink. This might take a while. You might even want to cancel your plans, which I apologize for in advance, but I had no other option," she said.

"You had no other option? What does that mean, exactly?"

Agnes removed her sunglasses, revealing what Clara suspected... a shiner on her upper cheekbone, covered with make-up.

"I don't have anywhere to stay, and I don't have a lot of money left in my account. I'm down to a quarter tank of gas... which is pretty pathetic, I know. But all I planned to do was make it from New York to your driveway, and well, here I am," she said.

Clara folded her arms, pacing by the sliding doors, noticing Agnes as she continued checking out the place.

"Who put the shiner on your face?" she asked.

"There's no sense getting into it now. He's in my past, where he belongs. Look, I know my showing up here was rather sudden and unannounced. I promise to come up with a plan to get out of your hair as quickly as possible, but for now, I need a place to stay, if it's all right with you."

Clara's phone buzzed several times as she continued staring at Agnes in disbelief.

"You want to stay here?" she asked.

"Yes, or at least I was hoping to. I couldn't think of anyone else who would take me in."

Again, the phone buzzed. This time she glanced over and noticed Mike's name flashing across the screen.

"Hold on a second," Clara said, while answering.

"Hello. Hi, Mike. Mm hmm, I know. I'm so sorry, I was preoccupied. I'm actually in a bit of a bind. My sister from New York just showed up. Is there any way I can take a rain check for tonight? I promise to make it up to you soon."

She continued talking.

"No, I'm okay. Really." She kept the call short and sweet, limiting herself from saying everything she was thinking in front of Agnes.

"Okay, babe. I'll call you before I head to bed."

Clara tapped the screen, ending the call, and stepped out of her heels.

"That explains why you're all dressed up. I'm really sorry. I screwed up your date night, didn't I?" she asked.

"Yes. But, more importantly, I need to get to the bottom of understanding what brought you here today. We haven't seen each other in ages, and this isn't quite the reunion I had in mind."

"I know. I never envisioned myself showing up at your front door, begging for a place to lay my head, either. The truth is, I wasn't even sure you and I would ever speak again. Not because I didn't want to, but because so much time had passed since mom and dad... passed away. Once they were gone, it seemed like everything went downhill from there," Agnes said.

Clara didn't disagree but continued listening.

"Why am I here, you ask? I guess after making a series of poor choices, I'm finally down on my luck. I'm probably getting everything I deserve in life.

How's the saying go? What goes around comes around..." She chuckled sarcastically.

"Nobody deserves to be abused, Agnes. No matter what you've done, it doesn't give anyone the right to hit you."

"That's what you think this is? Signs of abuse?" she asked, pointing to her bruise.

"He wasn't abusive. At least, not physically. This is the result of a last-minute scuffle on the way out the door. A scuffle with his new lady friend. She had the audacity to lunge toward me once she realized we were in a relationship. It always amazes me when I come across women who'd rather beat each other down instead of crucifying the real one at fault." She continued.

"Oh man, that's crazy."

"Yeah, tell me about it. I've never been much of a fighter, so you can only imagine what that entire scene looked like. It's all right. I'm fine and the shiner will heal. I just need to focus on getting my life back on track as expeditiously as possible, with minimal interruption to yours," she said.

Clara laughed slowly at first, then picked up the tempo, feeling trapped in the middle of a bad dream.

"What's so funny?"

"This is insane. I'm laughing just to keep from losing it. Just moments ago, I was preparing for a night out on the town. Agnes, you don't know how many times I contemplated picking up the phone to rekindle my relationship with you. I figured mom and dad would've wanted us to do better. We're family. But, somehow I always struggled, never quite feeling comfortable reaching out to you when I was at my lowest. I always thought it should've been under better circumstances," Clara said.

"But, you could've called."

"I chose not to, but I find it ironic how things worked out in the end. Earlier this year I was out of work and hopelessly trying to find my way. I was on the verge of having no place to go. It crossed my mind to reach out. But, I couldn't. Not after the way we ended things. You, on the other hand, show up at my doorstep just like it's nothing," Clara said.

Agnes walked over to the windows overlooking the boat slip. It hadn't gone unnoticed that she didn't respond, but Clara decided not to press the issue.

"You have yourself a nice place here. Looks like your worries of being unemployed and homeless are a thing of the past. You've come a long way from how we used to live growing up as little girls in New York," she said.

"Thank you. Although, it's nothing like you're probably thinking. I didn't gain all this on my own. But, enough about me... we have a lot of catching up to do before I can rest easy with you under my roof tonight. Does this loser you were with know where you are? Do you think he'll try to come after you?"

Agnes grunted in disgust, searching for the right words to convey her aggravation.

"We're fine. You don't have to worry about him. I didn't tell him where I was going, but I can confidently say he's harmless. More talk than anything else," she responded.

"Where did you meet this guy, anyway? Were you together long?"

"Long enough," she responded.

"I'm just curious. I promise, you'll get no judgment out of me. I've been with my share of losers and cheaters in my day. Take my ex, Keith, for example. You remember him. Man, I could tell you stories for days about how things ended with him. None of it was good," Clara said.

Agnes tossed her keys on the table, looking Clara straight in the eyes, captivating her attention.

"Clara, I guess there's no time like the present to share this with you. Might as well get it out of the way."

"Get what out of the way?" she asked.

Agnes was silent for what seemed like an eternity, creating an added level of awkwardness between the two.

"Well? What is it, already?" she asked.

Agnes took a deep breath.

"I just broke up with Keith. He's the reason I have this shiner on my face to begin with," she said.

"That's funny. You were dating a guy named

Keith? What are the odds?" Clara chuckled, totally misunderstanding what Agnes was trying to convey.

Agnes said nothing further. Instead, she stood waiting for her words to settle in.

"Isn't it odd?" Clara repeated, this time with a look of concern.

A moment passed before Clara's facial expression shifted completely.

"Agnes... how could you? Are you seriously standing before me, admitting that you were dating my ex-husband?"

Just like that, Clara's sister, whom she hadn't spoken to in years, was back in her life, ready to wreak havoc. The last time they spoke wasn't on good terms, and ten years later, they were right back where they started.

CHAPTER 2

"Welcome to Lighthouse Tours. How can I help you?" Mike said, welcoming his customers.

"Good morning, we're here to book an appointment for the fall lighthouse tour. I believe the flier said there's a special promotion running for the month of September."

"Yes, you've found the right place. Let me connect you with Ms. Mae. She's filling in for our office manager, Clara, today. She'd be more than happy to set you up with exactly what you're looking for."

Mae came from around the counter and greeted the new clients with a handshake, gladly willing to take them in.

In the back, Mike sat down with Brody, his employee and friend in charge of all things mechanical.

"Brody, my man. Please, have a seat. I hope you have good news for me today. I've got one boat down for the count here at the southern location, and another boat on its last leg over in North Beach. Our fall tours are selling like hotcakes, and folks are expecting me to deliver," he said.

The gentlemen settled in Mike's office with their usual legal pads, pencils tucked behind their ears, and coffee mugs.

"Have I ever let you down before? The boat over in North Beach is being repaired as we speak. As for the boat here, all it needs is a fine tune-up and a few minor adjustments, and she'll be good to go. Just as good as new," Brody said.

"Are you sure?"

"Yes. I'm positive. Are you all right, Mike? I'm happy to answer anything you want to know, but it's unlike you to be so concerned." Brody continued.

Mike placed his pencil down and propped his feet up on the desk.

"I know, Brody. I'm sorry, man. I guess I'm off my A-game this morning," he replied.

"Does this have anything to do with Clara? I know you planned on popping the question last night. How did it go?"

"It didn't go, at all. She canceled on me, which is so unlike Clara. In her defense, she said that her sister from New York showed up. I know they haven't seen each other in forever. I thought I'd give them some space, but talk about bad timing," Mike said.

"I'm sorry, man. That would put me in a mood, too. Have you talked to her today at all?"

"No. She said she would call me back last night before bed, but I haven't heard anything, other than Ms. Mae telling me she called in to take a personal day. I just have a strange feeling about this. I planned on giving her a couple of hours this morning, and if I don't hear from her, I'm going to call her by lunchtime."

Mike tossed his miniature basketball in the hoop, an activity he regularly engaged in when he was in a creative frame of mind. Today, it was more of a stress reliever.

"Listen, I'm sure whatever this is will blow over pretty quickly, and you can get back to your plans. Everything has been perfect with you two. There's nothing like knowing for certain when you've met the one." He claimed, making quotation marks with his fingers, emphasizing the one.

"You're right. Things have been pretty sweet between us. We met under the most unusual circumstances but look how far we've come in such a short period. We fit like a hand and glove, she's a constant cheerleader, and she helps run the southern office like a charm... as if it were her very own. What more could a guy ask for, right?" Mike asked.

"Exactly."

"I'm just going to talk to her, make sure every-thing's okay. After that, I'll put the proposal back in motion and pop the question as originally planned. Once that is behind me, my nerves can finally be at ease," he said.

"There he is. Now you're talking like the Mike Sanders I know."

They let out a little laugh, but for Mike, it was more like a sigh of relief.

"Thanks, Brody. I don't know where I'd be without you, brother. Whether it be on the business side of things or simply as a friend, you've always been there."

"Hey, I can say the same about you any day of the week. But, enough with all the sappy conversation. We've got work to do. If you have a few more min-utes, I'd like to go over plans for the new mechanic at North Beach," Brody said.

"Not a problem. What did you have in mind?"

Brody shared a couple of ideas on the training schedule he arranged for the new guy. Since Brody had been the only one in charge of the mechanics since the onset, it was only fitting that he would show him the ropes.

"I figured he could shadow me for a couple of weeks. I'll walk him through the procedures we have in place here and then bring him to North Beach as well. Ideally, I'd love to get him to a place where he can mainly oversee North Beach, and I stay here in Solomons. I wanted to check in with you and see if you had any additional thoughts on the matter," Brody said.

"Yeah, I think it sounds like a good idea, with one exception. Maybe as our newly promoted head manager of mechanics in charge of overseeing both locations, you can still pencil yourself in to come and visit North Beach... perhaps a couple of times a month?"

"Are you serious? Is this your way of saying I'm officially being promoted?" he asked.

"Yes, sir, not just in title, but the promotion comes along with a raise. I told you I was working on making this a reality. I'm just glad to finally be able to deliver."

"Mike, this is awesome. I promise you won't be sorry."

"Oh, I know it. You're skilled at what you do, and you've earned it. I just want you to train the new guy to do just as good of a job. I want Lighthouse Tours to have the best reputation in all of Northern and Southern Maryland, known for giving our clients a taste of nautical paradise. If we deliver on a five-star level, they'll refer us to their friends and keep coming back for more."

"Spoken like a true business owner." Brody smiled.

Mike peeked through the shades, noticing Jonathan outside, hosing down his boat, and Tommy pulling out with his first tour of the day.

"I'm going to check with Ms. Mae to see if she'd be interested in grabbing some brunch from the café for takeout. Do you want anything? This afternoon's schedule is jam-packed with tours, and I doubt I'll have time to grab anything to eat," Mike said.

"Count me in for my usual order. I'll leave a few dollars up at the front desk."

"Sounds good."

Brody pushed in his chair and almost made it out before he paused, leaning on the door frame.

"Hey, Mike."

"What's up?"

"Thank you, again. This promotion couldn't have come at a better time. You know it was always my dream to have a business of my own. But, when things fell through with that, you took me in and treated me like family. I'm invested in this place and forever grateful for all you've ever done for me. I mean it..." he said.

"You're welcome."

When Brody closed the door behind him, Mike nodded, feeling good about his decision. He then checked the clock, figuring he'd given Clara enough time, and anxiously dialed her telephone number.

Come on, Clara. Pick up, he muttered quietly to himself.

~

The morning rush quieted down at the cafe, leaving time for Ms. Mae to sit at the front counter to catch up with Mackenzie. Josh busied himself cleaning tables and Chloe, their part-time help, was out front receiving a shipment.

"Ms. Mae, I haven't seen you in a month of Sundays. How's everything?"

"I can't complain. Of course, if I did, no one would want to listen." She chuckled.

Mackenzie served Mae a glass of orange juice and took out her pad to jot down her order.

"Oh, there's no need for the notepad. We're going to put in our usual order for the office if you don't mind. I guess I could've called it in, but a little break every now and again never hurts," Mae said.

"The usual coming right up. I'm glad you decided to stop by. Clara talks about you and Jonathan all the time. How's married life treating you these days?"

Mae grinned.

"Oh, Jonathan and I are enjoying married life, if I say so myself. We still fuss at each other like we've been together for forty-plus years, but we're happy. That's what matters most, right?"

Mae leaned in closer, lowering her voice.

"And the intimate time is absolutely amazing. Who can complain about that?" she said.

Mackenzie's uncontrollable laughter could be

heard across the cafe. It wasn't uncommon to be taken off guard whenever Mae spoke.

"Ms. Mae, you're too much. I'm so glad to hear things are going well," Mackenzie said.

"Thank you. What about you and your friend... what's his name again?"

"Bill? He's the only guy I've been seeing off and on again," she responded.

"That's it, Bill. I don't like the idea of being on and off again. It's either one or the other. Are you two having a hard time getting along?"

"We get along when we're together, but I don't know, Ms. Mae. Lately, it seems like he's always busy. His daughter was in town visiting from college for the summer, but she should be back at school by now," she said.

"By the sound of things, I'll presume you didn't have a chance to meet her?"

"No. He seems rather protective about having his daughter involved in his personal life, which I can understand. But, it definitely made me feel extremely sensitive about introducing him to my Stephanie," Mackenzie answered.

"I don't blame you. How is sweet Stephanie doing?"

"She's wonderful. She's in second grade this year, she loves her teacher, and gets good grades. I'm pretty lucky to have her as my daughter. If only I can get my love life in order, maybe she'd actually have a steady father figure in her life again someday."

"Mackenzie, these things take time. If I were you, I'd start by addressing Bill and challenging him to be upfront with his feelings. He's a grown man, by now he should know if he's invested or not. Life's too short. You don't have time to waste," Mae said.

"You know what, Ms. Mae, I like the way you think. I'm going to take your advice to heart, but first, let me start by putting this order in with Chef Harold before Mike has to come looking for you."

"Thank you, dear. I'll be right here, shooting the breeze with Josh when he comes over. Tell Harold I said hello."

Mae smiled at a couple of customers she recognized from the Island and watched the big screen for a little while before Josh came to greet her.

"Ms. Mae, how are you... long time, no see," he said.

"Mackenzie said the same thing. Has it really been that long?"

"Yes, ma'am, too long for a lady who works right across the street," he said, giving her a hug.

"Aww, Josh, it's nice to know that I'm missed when I'm not around. I promise I'll be more diligent about coming in, even if it's just to say hello," she said.

"That's more like it. Oh, well, well, well... look at

what the cat dragged in. Another one who hasn't been visiting the café regularly, like she used to." Josh teased.

"Not now, Josh. I'm in no mood for it today," Clara said.

Ms. Mae turned around, surprised to see Clara standing right behind her. She had bags under her eyes, as if she'd missed a good night's sleep, and her hair was thrown together in a messy bun... the not-so-cute kind.

"Clara, what are you doing here on your day off?" Mae asked.

She hesitated, cautiously calculating how to answer.

"Let's just say I had to leave the house for a much-needed break from my sister. Is Mackenzie around by any chance?" she asked, looking around.

"What am I, chopped liver?" Josh teased.

"Joshua, I told you not today, and I mean it." She snarled somewhat playfully, but mostly serious.

He lifted his hands in surrender.

"Okay, touchy today, I see. I'll go get her. Have a seat. Make yourself comfortable."

Josh pressed his way through the double doors, disappearing to the back.

Mae gave Clara an unusual stare, not speaking a word at first, hoping Clara would explain herself.

"I take it that your visit with your sister isn't going so well?" Mae asked.

Clara pretended to be studying the menu, even though she knew the options by heart.

"It's okay. You don't have to tell me about it. I was just wondering if Mike knows you're here?" she asked.

"No, he doesn't, and please don't mention it. He left me a message, and I'd kind of like to be the first to talk to him, when I'm ready."

"Clara. What's wrong? What could be so terrible that would cause you to hide from Mike? Which... by the way, in case you hadn't noticed, you picked a pretty bad hiding spot. Lighthouse Tours is just a few feet away. He was really concerned about you calling in a personal day at the last minute. The least you could do is call him back," she said.

Mackenzie emerged untying her apron with Josh following closely behind. Chloe was wheeling in a few cartons of milk when she noticed the serious look on everyone's face and decided to keep moving.

"Call who? What did I miss?" Mackenzie asked.

She gave her best friend the once over, noticing Clara's messy appearance, which was so unlike her.

"Ooh, honey. What happened to you?"

Chloe returned from the back, placing Mae's order on the counter, laying the tab down beside the bag. Mae didn't budge, and Clara was fully aware that she had an audience.

"Guys, thanks for your concern. I had a long night, and I could really use a cup of coffee, and perhaps a little alone time to talk to Mack. I can always come back if this is a bad time," Clara said.

Josh and Chloe continued working while Ms. Mae placed her hand to her hip, appearing disappointed that Clara wasn't including her.

"Ms. Mae, I promise. Just give me some time to sort through things. If you could keep Mike occupied until I call him later today, that would be very helpful," she said.

"Are you sure you're all right?" Mae asked.

"Yes, I'll be fine."

Mae reached into her pocket and slid a bill across the counter.

"Keep the change," she said to Mackenzie, and then re-directed her attention toward Clara for the last time.

"Just know, I'm here if you need me, Darlin. You were kind enough to hold the fort down when Jonathan and I needed time off. So, if you need a few more days, just say the word."

"Thank you, Ms. Mae."

Once everyone cleared the front counter, Clara slid into her favorite chair and slumbered over the menu.

"Shall we make it black, today?" Mackenzie asked, referring to her coffee.

"If I was a drinker, I'd ask for a glass of whiskey," Clara said.

"But, since you're not, one cup of black coffee coming right up. Can I get you anything to eat?"

"Maybe something to go. I don't have much of an appetite."

Mackenzie poured fresh coffee from a carafe into Clara's mug. As she watched the steam rise, she wondered if Clara was ready to talk, but didn't want to push her.

"You picked the perfect day to take off from work. The kids are back in school, so it's nice and quiet. Plus, I'm almost certain if you throw a sweater on and head down by the shore, it will feel like a peaceful oasis. Maybe it will even help to clear your mind."

Mackenzie waited for a response... something ... anything would be better than the awkward silence, with occasional sipping sounds coming from Clara's mug.

"My sister showed up at my door last night." She acknowledged.

"Agnes? The sister you haven't seen in ten years?"

"Yep, the one and only."

"Isn't that something? I always wondered if the two of you would ever reunite," Mackenzie said.

"Well... wonder no more. We have officially reunited."

Mackenzie watched as Clara continued cradling

her mug. She held up the carafe, offering to top her off, and Clara graciously accepted.

"I take it your reunion didn't go so well?"

"Ha, that's an understatement. I won't get into the details. Not in here, at least. But let's just say I was a lot better off prior to her arrival. A lot better off." Clara repeated

"You're killing me here. I know you want to talk or else you wouldn't have come down here to see me. You've got a whole beach in your backyard if all you wanted to do was quietly reflect," Mackenzie said.

"Oh, trust me. I've been on the beach since sunrise, contemplating the many ways I could elude my current reality, but I couldn't come up with anything. So, I ended up here, thinking maybe you'd have time to take a break and go for a walk. More than anything, I just needed a change in scenery. If only for a little while."

"Josh is about to leave for an hour for his dentist appointment, and Chloe is handling the deliveries. I can't leave right now, but we can grab a booth and I'll be an ear for you."

Clara glanced around, noticing a few customers from the area, some who knew her from Lighthouse Tours.

"It's okay. Let's save it for when you're off. Maybe you can call me later on?" she asked.

"Are you sure?"

"I'm positive. Now... tell me something uplifting

to help take my mind off things. Where's Bill these days? You two planning anything special this week?"

Mackenzie cracked a smile, but it wasn't a happy one.

"There must be a sign on my forehead today that says ask me about my love life. First Ms. Mae and now you. Except the only problem is there's nothing to tell. He seems to be focused on other things. It's like we've reached some sort of stalemate or something."

"No way, I'm not buying it. Just two weeks ago you were still on cloud nine after one of your dates. He didn't have a change of heart that fast," Clara said.

Mackenzie shrugged her shoulders.

"I can't put my finger on it, but something is off. His daughter is back at college so it can't be that. I don't know. Mae said I should talk to him, and I probably will when the time is right."

"There's no time like the present. Know who you're dealing with before things get too serious. You have to be ever so careful with who you trust. Including your own flesh and blood," Clara mumbled.

Mackenzie drew her eyebrows together, trying to read between the lines.

"Okay, that does it. Hey, Josh. What time is your appointment again?" she yelled across the café.

"Not for another hour from now. Take your walk.

You got time," he replied, revealing that he'd been listening in.

Mackenzie rolled her eyes.

"I'll tell you one doctor he doesn't need to visit... his ears are working just fine." She laughed.

"Come on. Grab your purse and follow me. We have some catching up to do."

CHAPTER 3

$\mathcal{M}$ackenzie led Clara as far up the road away from the other businesses as possible. The sound of the seagulls and the fresh smell of water overwhelmed their senses, quietly leading them before they began speaking.

Clara stopped abruptly and opened up about her troubles.

"After all this time had passed, I thought surely, if Agnes and I ever reconnected, it would be for good reasons. Never in a million years did I think she'd show up at my door, confessing she'd been in a relationship with my ex," she said.

Mackenzie's mouth dropped open as she struggled to find the right words to console her friend.

"What?"

"Yes, they've been seeing each other for the last

four or five years. According to her, he never revealed that we were still legally married until recently," Clara said.

"Is she aware that he was in town, seeking your inheritance, which then led to the divorce?"

"She claims she didn't know. I asked her why she would ever entertain getting involved with him to begin with. It just happened, was all she could say. What a likely story... she said they ran into each other when things were hard and they were lonely. Give me a break."

"Unbelievable," Mackenzie said, trying to process everything as they continued to walk.

"I swear, if it wasn't because she showed up with a black and blue eye with no place to go, I may have been inclined to slam the door in her face."

"Did he hit her?" Mackenzie asked.

"No, but his new lady friend did. I guess she was defending her man. If only she knew... Agnes may have some twisted ways about her, but she's no fighter. The more I think about it, I can totally see how this whole thing happened. My sister has always gravitated toward those who could easily play with her emotions, and she can be naïve. Except this time, it finally caught up to her. She has no money, no place to go, and she had to come looking for me, out of pure desperation. How pathetic."

Mackenzie stopped at a nearby bench and sat, crossing her legs over. She had the sternest expression on her face, questioning everything about Agnes and what was to come of this.

"I'm having a hard time digesting that you're here talking to me while she's at your house," Mackenzie said.

"I needed to get out and take a breather. It was too much to handle. I literally buried Keith in my past with the final divorce papers a couple of months ago. I know I should've acted on it years ago but you know my reasons for not doing so... I needed to get away from him and start a brand new life. It's the exact thing I'm trying to do with Mike... start fresh and move forward." Clara complained.

"I understand that, honey. You didn't ask for this, but don't you think it would be wise to go back to the house and sort this out with your sister? Heck, can you even trust the woman after all these years? Who's saying she's telling you the whole story? What if she knew about Keith coming to Solomons Island, trying to threaten you for money? Since that whole thing backfired on him, what if they're teaming up for part two of their little scheme, sending her this time to do some damage?" Mackenzie implied.

"Mack, thank you for looking out for me. Trust me, I considered all these things and lost a lot of sleep trying to cover every angle. But, even if there was an ounce of truth to it, she can't do any more damage than what's already been done. Besides, I never leave anything of importance in the house. Everything is in a safe where it ought to be. I'm more concerned about my emotional well-being than anything else. Do you realize how mortified I am? To think we come from the same bloodline. How can I even begin to explain this to Mike? Especially after everything with the inheritance and the divorce. He will not want to be associated with someone like me." Clara swiftly smeared a tear away from her cheekbone.

"I think you're being a little hard on yourself, and you're not giving Mike a fair chance. What do you plan to do? Avoid him all week?" Mackenzie asked.

"No. I'll call him later on, but I need to figure out what to do with my sister first. My parents would roll over in their grave if I kicked her out when she has nowhere to go."

"Better you than me, girl. Better you than me." She grunted.

A couple strolled by, riding two vintage bicycles, laughing playfully with one another. Clara watched them, recalling that same feeling of pure joy in her lifeless than twenty-four hours ago. She wiped away another tear.

"Come on, now. Whatever happens, you will not let this thing defeat you. It's a temporary setback. Every family has a rotten apple or two. You're going to be fine. I suggest at some point, once the dust has settled, you allow me to meet Ms. Agnes. If you introduce her to the rest of us, she'll see how protective we are of you. We won't stand for any nonsense, Clara," Mack said.

"That would assume that I'm okay with being seen with her in public. I don't know about that. I love Solomons, but news travels way too fast around here for me."

"It's a small island, but the people around here have nothing but love for one another. Please don't let this influence you to return to the secluded life you once lived."

McKenzie waited for a response and pressed the issue when Clara didn't seem to react.

"Okay, I'll work on it. You just have to give me time. This is a tough pill to swallow. I still have to go back to the house and look her in the eye. This isn't easy."

The ladies walked back toward the café, Clara deviating to her car and McKenzie waiting for her friend to pull off before returning inside.

Back at the house Agnes stood in an oversized t-shirt, hovering over the stove, sampling something she was stirring with a ladle. Clara didn't know whether to be grateful that she was at least making herself useful in the kitchen or annoyed at how comfortable she was.

"There you are. I was wondering if you ran away,

leaving me with this huge place and such a sweet little dog," she said, bending to pet Holly.

Clara tossed her purse on the counter, not at all impressed by her comment.

"I left to grab some fresh air."

"How much fresh air does one need? I saw you walking on the beach earlier this morning," Agnes said.

"And, I may need to go for walks every morning to help keep my sanity. Either way, I don't have to answer to you about my whereabouts."

Clara removed her sweater, folding it neatly over the chair in front of her.

"We need to talk... perhaps go over some ground rules... make sure we're clear on a few things." She continued.

"I'm listening. Don't mind my back, I need to keep my eye on this clam chowder I'm throwing together. It's a little chilly out here by the water. I thought I'd search through your fridge to see if I could throw together something warm to stick to our bones."

"You didn't have to do that."

"I know, but I figured I needed to start earning my keep around here. If not, I knew you'd come down on my case just like mom used to. You guys were always two peas in a pod in that respect. I blame it on the type-A personalities," Agnes said.

Oh no, she didn't, Clara thought to herself.

"That's an interesting comment to make given all that mom did for us. Our parents worked their fingers to the bone trying to provide a nice life for us and all you can seem to come up with is some sarcastic remark about a personality type?" She continued.

Agnes turned off the burner, placed the ladle down, and inspected the soup before turning around to address Clara.

"Here we go. I've been waiting for this moment."

"What moment?" Clara asked.

"The moment of judgment coming from my older sister. The one who can do no wrong."

Clara carefully calculated her response, weighing her options, not ruling out the idea of putting a time limit on how long she could stay.

"Let's tread carefully here, remembering that you're the one who came knocking on my door, and not the other way around. Starting today, you can move your things out of the guest room and down to the basement, in my old sleeping quarters. I'll see to it you have sheets and whatever else you need before dinner. You're welcome to anything to eat, but be mindful that I live here, too. Oh yeah, and my boyfriend comes around frequently, so there will be no walking around the house half-dressed."

"You have a boyfriend?" Agnes interrupted, wearing a smirk on her face.

Clara mentally counted to ten and exhaled.

"And finally, I'll give you about a week to get your

thoughts together. Then, we need to sit down and layout a plan to get you on your feet as soon as possible," she said.

"Why? Have I already overstayed my welcome? You have all this square footage. Is it really going to kill you to…"

"Stop… right… there. You have yet to thoroughly explain yourself, and you definitely don't seem remorseful for showing up unannounced. On top of that, I have to tell ya… this presumptuous attitude of yours better disappear immediately if you want any help from me. Are we clear?" Clara asked in a stern voice.

"Yes." Agnes looked up, trying to slow down the water forming in her eyes.

"I'm sorry," she said, quickly wiping her face.

"You're right. I'll do better. I didn't mean to come off like a jerk. It's just… I don't know what to say or how to be around you, Clara. Call it a defense mechanism, I guess. It's hard getting past my pride and coming here like this. Now that I'm standing in front of you, my heart says to do the right thing… cook… clean… do anything to carry my weight. But, I open my mouth and fall right back in line with where we left off from ten years ago. I swear I didn't mean any harm. Please, give me another chance."

Clara pulled out a chair at her kitchen table and plopped down, letting out a sigh.

"Okay, you want another chance. Why don't you

start by telling me why you thought dating Keith was a good idea? What did you really think would come of it, Agnes? Did your conscience ever get the best of you with that decision?" Clara asked, wearing her best poker face.

"I was honest when I told you we were vulnerable... lonely... and even-"

"Desperate?" Clara asked.

Agnes waited a moment.

"Yes, in hindsight... I guess that, too," she said.

"I remember the day we ran into each other clearly, like it was yesterday.

"I was standing in line at the sandwich shop, the one off Adams Street near the town center. I remember hearing the voice of an elderly woman behind me asking someone to help her read the menu. She said something about forgetting her glasses at home. The male voice that responded to her sounded so familiar. I turned around, and there he was. He asked if he could join me for lunch, sat down, and we caught up for hours. Keith told me he hadn't seen or heard from you in years, and call me crazy, but we were there for each other. I had just come out of a tough relationship, and..." She fell silent, trying to find a tactful way to explain things, not wanting to make Clara mad.

"He needed someone to lie in bed with at night?" she responded.

"Clara. Come on. It wasn't like that. We took our

time, talking and getting to know each other at first. We talked for a couple of months before anything developed. Even then, I was almost at the point of not being able to cover my next month's rent, and he certainly wasn't having an easy time at his job. I guess we just ended up leaning on each other, probably for the wrong reasons, but I swear... it's not like there was some instant attraction with total disregard for you."

Clara rolled her eyes.

"Funny how the tables have turned. Had you ever considered how you would explain this if you ever saw me again? Or maybe you just assumed that would never happen? I mean, what if you'd gotten married and had babies together? Ugh. The thought of it just makes me sick," she said.

Agnes joined Clara at the table, not quite able to look her sister in the eye but knowing how much a heartfelt response was needed.

"I was wrong, Clara, and there's absolutely nothing I can say to make things right. I know you're probably thinking the only reason I'm apologizing is because I need a place to stay, but trust me, the feelings of guilt have been haunting me long before now. What I did was wrong, and I'm sorry. As for my attitude, my attire around the house, and anything else you request of me, I'm more than willing to comply," Agnes said, cautiously slipping one hand over Clara's to which she withdrew.

"I don't know that I'll ever fully understand it,

but I appreciate you taking the time to explain. I've got an awful headache. I'm going to grab your linens from upstairs and then lie down for a while."

Within the hour, Clara was lying on her pillow, stained with tears, feeling the burden of having her sister back in her life. She committed to napping for a short while with plans to wake up refreshed and ready to call Mike.

~

"Clara," a voice whispered.

"Clara, over here."

In her dreams Clara saw Mike walking toward her on the beach slowly, then picking up the pace in anticipation of embracing. He was close enough to touch her but stopped, distracted by Agnes, standing in her bathing suit, showing off her hourglass figure.

"Clara, it's me, Mike," he said

She jolted out of her sleep, realizing it hadn't been a dream. Mike was standing over her in his business attire, gently brushing her hair out of the way.

"It's me. I didn't mean to frighten you. It's okay," he said, kissing her on the cheek.

She looked around, checking to see that she was still in her bedroom, where she last fell asleep.

"You're in the right place." He chuckled.

"Your sister let me in. I feel terrible for waking you up, but after twelve missed phone calls, I couldn't take it anymore. I had to come see for myself that you were okay," he said.

She checked to make sure she wasn't drooling.

"No, don't apologize. I had every intention of calling you back before now. I must've overslept," she responded.

There was a light tap on the door, which was already slightly ajar.

"I don't want to interrupt. Just making sure everything is okay up here," Agnes said, while remaining in the hall.

"We're fine, I just overslept, that's all."

"Okay, I'll be downstairs if you need me." She closed the door, allowing them a little privacy.

"So, that's the sister you've been telling me about all this time, huh?" Mike said.

"Yep, that's her. In the flesh."

"Man, from what I can tell, you must've had some kind of night. It's not like you to not call me back. I started to worry about you, Clara," Mike said.

"Aww, everything is fine."

"Really?"

"Maybe not everything, but I'm safe, and there's nothing for you to worry about. I owe you an apology for not being more responsible to reach out sooner."

Mike removed his shoes and crawled into bed with her. Once adjusted in an upright position against the pillows, he opened his arms, inviting her to lie beside him.

"You know you can talk to me about anything, right?" he asked.

"I know..."

Minutes passed as Clara continued to lie on his chest, resting peacefully like a baby.

"Clara, it's not like you to keep to yourself and bottle everything inside. Whatever is going on with the two of you. She seemed nice enough when she greeted me at the door, and even a few minutes ago when she came to check on you. Things can't be that terrible, can they?" he asked.

"Don't be fooled by a few acts of kindness here and there. Her core is still just as rotten as ever," she said.

"Whoa. Okay, then. Didn't see that coming, but it's a start. Should I be concerned about her being here in the house with you? I can stay if you want me to."

"That's not a good idea," she snapped, then reconsidered her actions.

"Sorry, I was just trying to look out for you, that's all."

He pulled her in closer, combing his fingers through her hair.

"We can talk about this when you're ready," he whispered.

Clara glanced up at Mike, wearing the look of hurt and despair in her eyes.

"Thank you for understanding."

"I'd do anything for you. Hopefully, you know that by now."

He kissed her, graduating from a soft peck to a more passionate kiss, hoping to help her forget everything. She clung to him momentarily, but thoughts of her sister still continued to linger in the back of her mind.

CHAPTER 4

Mackenzie strolled beside Bill along the campgrounds at the local fair. She was sorry she wore her new jeans with the warmer than usual September weather, but they were fitted, showing off her figure, something that might look appealing to Bill. Her daughter, Stephanie, was invited to a sleepover, making it the perfect afternoon for a date, and hopefully a chance for them to reconnect.

"If Stephanie were here, she'd lose her mind over the cotton candy." She laughed, trying to strike up conversation with Bill.

"You should bring her back here before the fair is over... that way you can enjoy a little mother-daughter time. I'm sure she'd like that," he said.

"I plan on it. Some activities never get old to her, and this is one of them."

They continued strolling, occasionally stopping by a vendor to check out the goods for sale.

"I was kind of hoping you'd want to tag along with us some time so you could actually meet Steph. She's a sweet girl. I think the two of you would get along very well," she said.

"Yeah, my only issue is I barely get time off these days. The mere fact that I got off today was a miracle. I almost called to reschedule with you so I could get some shut-eye, but I didn't want to disappoint."

Mackenzie's eyes shifted to the ground, feeling uncertain of how to take his comment.

"I understand. If the boss is giving out opportunities to work overtime hours, that's not something you want to miss. After all, you have a girl in college. That's a hefty bill, I'm sure."

"Tell me about it," he replied.

They continued walking for a while. Mackenzie realized they really weren't engaging in the festivities or even grabbing a bite to eat, which made her even more curious about what was running through his mind.

"I'll bet you miss your daughter after having her here during the summer. Have you guys talked much since she's been back?" she asked.

"It was definitely an enjoyable time. She's your typical college student. Sleeps in a lot and is a live wire at night. She definitely reminds me of how I used to be when I was that age. We talk, maybe once or twice a month, now that we're back to our regular routine."

"I see."

He finally stopped by a food stand, glancing over the menu.

"Would you like to grab a couple of hot dogs?" he asked.

"Sure, who comes to the fair without indulging in a hot dog or two?" She smiled.

When they were done eating, they remained in their seat, people watching, not saying much other than an occasional reaction whenever someone landed in a dunking tank.

"Bill, what's going on here?" she asked in a solemn voice.

"A bunch of idiots are getting soaking wet in a dunking booth. Of all the things to do here, that wouldn't be at the top of my list," he said.

"No... that's not what I'm referring to, although I can't say I disagree. I'm talking about with us. This doesn't quite feel like a date."

"What does it feel like?" he asked.

She secretly wished he didn't make her spell everything out.

"Like something is wrong, but neither of us wants to say what it is."

He let out a sigh.

"It's probably the exhaustion kicking in."

"Bill... it's okay. You don't have to do this. Feelings change. You can come out and tell me the truth. I can handle it," she said.

He continued looking straight ahead, avoiding eye contact at all costs.

"I met someone on the job. It's nothing serious or anything, so please don't assume the worst. We're just friends." He confessed.

"But, you like her... and you desire to be more than just friends?"

He nodded his head in agreement.

"Well, okay. I'm glad that's behind us. I suspected something was up. It's kind of sad you didn't feel comfortable enough to tell me on your own," she said.

"What could I say, Mackenzie? Heck, I wasn't even sure I wanted to discuss it at all. I kept saying to myself, what if this is nothing? Do you know how terrible I would feel about hurting you?" he asked.

She cocked her head back and let out laughter with an air of sarcasm.

"A woman knows how to read between the lines, Bill. Whether or not you brought it up, all the signs were there. We've been seeing each other long enough to know the difference. If you were really that into me, you'd want to meet my girl and you'd want me to meet your daughter. Or at least you'd talk about it in terms of the near future. Then there's all the withdrawn behavior and the overtime hours... at least now it all makes sense," she said.

He shifted from his position to address her.

"Mack, I'm sorry. You know me. I'm a decent guy. I never intended to hurt you."

She held her finger up.

"You didn't hurt me, Bill. You tried to insult my intelligence while you were figuring things out, but you didn't hurt me. It's all good. I want you to be happy, and I deserve to be happy, too."

"Do you mean that?" he asked.

She sat back, crossing her legs.

"I do. Life's too short. If you like the girl, pursue it... see where it leads," she said.

"You mean, you're not the least bit angry at me right now?" he asked.

"Oh, don't get me wrong. I've already considered smacking you at least once, but my mother raised a lady. So, lucky for you we're going to part ways peacefully this afternoon."

"Dear Lord, thank you," he said, letting out a sigh of relief.

They both chuckled before settling down.

"Just do me a favor, will you?" she asked.

"What's that?"

"Be straightforward with the woman should you have a change of heart. You're old enough to know better." She scolded.

"Lesson learned, I promise."

The conversation on the way home was minimal at best, both treading carefully given they'd just broken up. Mackenzie rode home in the passenger seat, realizing it would probably be the last time they'd be together. Maybe even the last time they'd see each other, if Bill avoided coming to the café.

Early the next morning, Jonathan hosed his boat down, whistling to the music playing by the dock. He toweled down parts of the interior, recalling how his father used to do the same after every family boat ride when he was young.

Mae appeared from behind, overhearing him, reminiscing out loud.

"Talking to yourself, dear?" she asked.

"Not quite. I was recalling how dad used to take the family on boat rides during the summer. It was our version of a staycation. Somehow, he turned our little tours around the bay into a great big adventure."

"I'll bet he's the reason you love boating so much," she said.

"He sure is. He taught me everything I know about navigating the sea and about fishing, of course."

"Jonathan," she said, looking deep in thought.

"Yes, Mae?"

"If it weren't for Mike giving us this opportunity with Lighthouse Tours, do you think you'd still be planted solely in Maryland?"

"Without a doubt. Don't tell me you're thinking about wanting to live elsewhere, Mae," he said.

"Not at all. I was just wondering if you could ever see yourself sailing and visiting other places, especially since you love nautical life so much. Who knows, maybe you'd even consider purchasing a boathouse?"

Jonathan put his broom down, facing her to ensure he was hearing right. She'd always been known for her routines and having a particular way she lived her life. He found it to be odd that she would even entertain the idea of living on a boat.

"I may have dreamt of it a time or two, but now that we're married, I laid all those dreams aside, putting your wants and needs first, Mae. Residing on a boat doesn't seem like something you'd ever want to do. I always thought you were more of a small cottage kind of woman, enjoying your rocking chair on the front porch and gardening, of course," he responded.

She smiled.

"You know me well, Jonathan, but with everything we've been through this past year with our relationship, and almost breaking things off, and me struggling back then with the idea of change... it taught me a lot about myself. I'm still learning more and more every day."

"Like what? How particular you are about where shoes go, or the time of the evening you'd prefer for the house to be quiet?" He teased, laughing a bit more than Mae would've cared for.

"Oh, hush, Jonathan. You know what I mean," she said.

"Yes, I do. Continue. I'm all ears."

"I work hard, but I don't play hard enough. You don't have that problem. You're so much more of a free spirit than I am, and I love that about you. It kind of has me thinking, maybe I need to learn how to live a little more, before it's too late."

"Too late? Mae, how many times do we need to have this conversation about your best years being ahead of you? It's not too late for anything," he said.

"Mm hmm. I'm old enough to consider these things, that's all I'm trying to say."

"I guess it's wonderful that you're open to considering new things, Mae. But, living on a boat?"

"Well, it's probably not a permanent solution, but would you consider us purchasing a boat to travel with? This way we'd still have the cottage when we're working, and we could set sail when we have time off to get out there and explore a little."

Jonathan lifted Mae off her feet and spun her around, kissing her repeatedly before placing her back down.

"Wait a minute. Before I get too excited. Is this

some sort of passing idea or are you serious as in ready to move forward on this?" he asked.

"I wouldn't have brought it up if I wasn't serious. I figured, now that your old place is sold, a new boat would be a fraction of the cost, and it might be something you'd want to invest in."

"Mae, I could pick you up and spin you around all over again," he said with an expression of joy.

Mae held her hand out against his chest, stopping him before he followed through with it, laughing the entire time.

"Jonathan, we're at work. Save the excitement for later on tonight. Then, we can snuggle up and talk more about our plans," she said.

"Don't you threaten me with a good time, woman. You know I'll take you up on the offer. We don't have to wait for tonight. We can run home for some snuggle time at lunch." He teased.

"Jonathan!"

"All right, I'll cool down. But, seriously, I love the idea, Mae. Thank you for being open to this. I can see us now... planning trips, setting sail across the sea, and making sweet memories together. Memories that go far beyond giving tours here on Solomons Island," he said.

"I can see it, too. Do you know what else I can see?"

"No, but from the look on your face I can tell it's something good," he said.

"Oh, it is. Remember the impromptu date you planned for us with an overnight stay on a yacht, sailing across Chesapeake Bay?"

"Yes."

"Do you remember what we did that night, under the stars?" She smiled.

"Woman, if you want me to behave, you better get back to work, and run fast if you know what's best for you."

"I will, but this conversation is not over," she replied.

"No, it is not. We're just getting started."

Back inside, Mae returned to find Mike stacking and shifting boxes around in the supply room. She watched him for several minutes, trying to figure out what he was working up such a sweat over.

It wasn't until he attempted to unstack a pile he just stacked that prompted her to interrupt him.

"Mike."

He jumped, startled at the sound of her voice.

"Ms. Mae, good morning. I didn't see you standing there," he said.

"Apparently not. You were too busy stacking and re-stacking to notice me," she said, peering into one of the open boxes.

"I don't think I've ever seen so many boxes of

copy paper before. Are you working on a special project of some sort?" she asked.

"No, it was a mistake. Jan, the secretary at the North Beach office, had a bunch of these sent here by accident. It's no big deal. Figured I'd try to store everything out of Clara's way until we figure out what to do with all this."

"Ah ha, I see. I guess that makes sense."

She paused for a long moment, discerning there was more to his busy behavior than a misplaced shipment.

"Is everything all right with you two?" she asked.

"With me and Clara? Sure, things couldn't be better. What makes you ask a question like that?"

"I've known you for a long time, Mike. Jonathan and I both recognize when something isn't right with you. One of the telltale signs is your over-indulgence in things that aren't important. Like fiddling around with boxes of copy paper, for example," she said, picking up a ream and displaying it before him.

"If it's not relationship troubles, it's something. The question is, are you going to be honest with me and come out with it, or do I have to pry it out of you?" she asked.

He took a seat on one of his stacks.

"Sometimes I forget how well the two of you know me. I've never been good at keeping a poker face, and I have a bad habit of wearing my feelings on my sleeve," he replied.

"It's not the worst thing in the world. What's bothering you?"

Mike viewed Mae and Jonathan as more than employees. They were trustworthy, would do anything for him, and had become more like family members over the years.

He glanced toward the door.

"Did the two of you break up or something?" she asked.

"No, of course not."

"Well, then, come out with it already. What's bothering you?" she asked impatiently.

"Without going into the specifics, let's just say I was planning something special for Clara, but her sister's impromptu visit sort of put a damper on things."

"I figured it was related to her sister. I never heard the details, but I've had a bad vibe about her arrival ever since I ran into Clara at the café yesterday."

"You ran into her at the café yesterday?" he asked.

"Oops. I guess I wasn't supposed to say that. Clara didn't want to upset you, and she promised she was going to call you later that day. It's no big deal. She needed time with her best friend. You know how tight they are. It meant nothing, I promise."

Mike looked disappointed.

"Interesting. I waited for hours to hear from her

before finally going over there to check on her," he said.

"Mike, don't do that. Clara adores you. Her sister's reemergence has obviously touched a nerve of some sort. Give her a little time. She'll come around."

"I guess you're right. Do you mind if I pick your brain about something?" he asked.

"Go for it. I'm all ears."

"You've been around to observe our progress. You know how Clara and I met, and you know everything about me and how I make decisions."

"Right," she said.

"Do you think Clara and I have been moving too fast with the progression of our relationship?"

"No, for heaven's sake, what would make you say that? You two have been a perfect match ever since the day she backed her car into yours. She's wife material and completely different from that other one you were with... what was her name again?" Mae chuckled.

"Ms. Mae, there's no need to go there. I get your point. What I'm asking is... could you see us together for the long haul? I respect your opinion, and I'd really like to hear your take on this. I probably should've asked you this before now, but do you think I'm rushing into things like a hopeless fool in love?" he asked.

"You're planning on proposing, aren't you?"

Mike cracked a smile, revealing his bright white

teeth and his intentions. Mae knew that look in his eyes. She'd seen it twice before in her lifetime. The first from her late husband, and the second time from Jonathan.

"Ahh, I see what this is all about. There's no way you'd be acting like this if you were just talking about dating. Am I right?"

"Yes, ma'am. I'd like to propose. I went as far as making the plans, purchasing the ring, and was ready to pop the question, but then all this happened, giving me extra time to reflect."

Mae gave him a look of disapproval.

"Once you've arrived at the point of buying a ring, your mind should be made up without wavering, young man. Now, do you want to marry the girl or not?" she asked.

"Yes, without a doubt. And, to be clear, I'm really not wavering about Clara. She's the perfect woman for me. It's just-"

"What?"

"With her sister showing up and her being really upset, it has me realizing that I really don't know a lot about Clara's family. Outside of the stories she's told here and there, I mainly know Clara Covington from Solomons Island. The woman who started a new life when she moved here ten years ago, and even then, she was running away from her past. Maybe it wouldn't hurt for me to press a little and get to know

Clara Covington from New York... that part of her life counts for something. Right?" he asked.

Mae shrugged her shoulders, feeling dissatisfied with his reasoning, hoping he wouldn't change his mind altogether.

CHAPTER 5

Clara stood in the hallway, overhearing the conversation with Mike and Ms. Mae. She paused a few steps away from his door, hearing him stress the importance of getting to know Clara Covington from New York. It made her feel sick to her stomach hearing the words. It was the very part of her she wanted to bury for good. Even worse, she wondered why he was sharing this with Mae instead of being upfront with her.

"Clara, do you have a moment? I was hoping to submit a few purchase items for approval," Brody asked, startling her from behind.

"Brody, uh sure, sorry. I didn't hear you coming," she said, taking the papers from him and quickly returning to the front desk.

"No worries, I wasn't sure if you were thinking

about going in the storage room or just deep in thought, but I figured I'd grab you while I could."

"That's perfectly fine. Okay, what do we have here? More boat equipment. Got it. If you give me ten minutes max, I'll process these and get you an approval form," she said.

"Perfect. I'll pick up the form on my way up to the North Beach office."

Brody lingered a while longer, flipping through some papers and tapping his pen on the counter space behind her.

"Brody, can I help you with anything else?" she asked.

"I'm sorry. Was I being too loud? I have this silly habit of fidgeting... sometimes I don't even realize when it's happening."

He scratched his signature on a few documents, sipped his coffee loudly, and then began tapping his foot.

"Have you seen Ms. Mae around?" he asked.

"I think she's in the back, talking to Mike. You can head on back there if you'd like."

"Oh, no. I'll just hang out here. It's not a problem."

Clara laid her pen down.

"Brody, what's on your mind?" she asked, trying her best not to show how irritated she was.

He looked around.

"Who? Me?"

"No, the other Brody sitting around making tapping sounds for no good reason," she said.

He laughed, sounding a little nervous.

"All right, you got me. I have a question for you, but I was hoping we could keep it between us. I don't want everyone in my business if we can help it," he said.

Clara could tell he was trying to muster up the courage so she eased up a bit.

"Sure, what's up?"

"It's about your friend, Mackenzie."

"What about her?" It didn't take long to realize this was personal.

"I was wondering if she's still seeing that guy, the lumberjack? The word around town is they parted ways. How is she doing with the breakup?" he asked.

"What breakup? She didn't mention anything to me about it. Then again, I've been a little preoccupied these days, so maybe I'm out of the loop. Why are you asking?"

"I don't know... just curious, I guess."

His response didn't sound so convincing. How often does a guy ask about the details of a woman's relationship unless his heart is involved?

"Are you interested in her?"

"Whoa, whoa. You don't have to go around saying that so loud. Rumors travel fast," he replied.

Clara knew McKenzie wasn't feeling good about her last date with Bill, but she couldn't speak to their current status. She glanced at Brody, considering what she knew about him. He was a quiet homebody; he was kind to children, just didn't have any of his own, he was well respected on the island, and hardworking. *Why hadn't Brody and Mackenzie considered each other before now?* she thought.

"Brody, there's a difference between a rumor and a fact. The truth is, you like her... don't you?" she asked.

"I may have noticed her a time or two."

"And you've never said anything to her?" Clara asked.

"In case you hadn't noticed, I'm more of a quiet, low-key kind of guy. Striking up a conversation with women isn't exactly my forte."

She nodded, seeing how that could be the case. At least it was the case for her when she first moved to Solomons.

"Look, if you think it's a bad idea, I trust your judgment. I just thought if she'd give lumberjack a chance, maybe an old mechanic like myself might have a shot," he said, slowly backing away.

"I'll let you get back to your paperwork. I can stop by later for those approval sheets." He continued.

Clara was tempted to take him up on his offer, given how distracted she was after overhearing Mike talking to Mae. But Brody was a nice guy and if

Mackenzie would be interested, the least she could do was investigate.

"Brody, wait. Let me see what I can find out. And for the record, you need to stop selling yourself short. You're a great catch... if not for Mackenzie, then someone else. You just have to get out there and let your personality shine, that's all."

"Yeah, that's what they say. Only problem is I'm the textbook definition of an introvert." He tugged his baseball cap down further, covering his eyebrows. "Either way, thanks for your help," he said, proceeding to leave before turning around one last time.

"If you wouldn't mind, can we-"

"Keep this between us?" she asked.

"Exactly."

"Sure, no problem."

"Thanks, I'll see you later," he replied.

Once Brody exited to the back, a customer entered, approaching the front desk. Clara noticed Mae grabbing coffee and Mike walking around in the back, acting as if everything was normal.

"Good morning, welcome to Lighthouse Tours. How may I help you?" she asked.

"Hi, my husband and I want to plan a tour for my in-laws who will visit in a couple of weeks. I was wondering if you had a brochure or information I could take home and share?" she asked.

"Absolutely. I'd strongly encourage you to consider our tour of Annapolis. Everyone raves about it, and I can personally say the views are to die for." Clara explained.

"Really? Well, I'm sold. My in-laws love sailing, so I know they'll be happy. How about I book the tour now, and if my husband wants to make any changes we can call back if needed?"

"Perfect. Let me pull up the schedule on the computer."

The phone rang amid scheduling the tour. It was Agnes, apologetically, asking for a couple of minutes of Clara's time.

"Agnes, hold on a moment. I'm wrapping things up with a customer," she said, placing her on hold.

"Okay, you're all set. Here's your receipt and con- firmation of your date and time. Plan to arrive early. Our tours usually depart on schedule."

"Thank you."

"Mm hmm, take care." Clara watched as the customer left before reconnecting to Agnes on line one.

"Are you still there?"

"Yes, I'm here."

"What are you doing, calling me at work? This better be an emergency, Agnes."

"It is... somewhat. I was wondering if on the way in you could stop by the grocery store and pick up some crackers and ginger ale?"

"What's wrong?" Clara asked.

"I'm feeling a little under the weather, but it's

nothing I can't get past. If I could have those items for later on that would be very helpful."

"Sure, crackers... ginger ale... anything else?" she asked.

"No, that should do it. Thanks, Clara."

"All right. Feel better."

She hung up to the sight of Brody and Mike wheeling out a couple of hand trucks stacked with boxes.

"Brody, I'll have your form ready for you in two minutes if you want to come grab it before you leave."

"Sure, I'll be right back," he said.

Mike stopped at her desk, greeting her with a quick peck on the cheek.

"It's nice to see you back in the swing of things. Is everything okay with you and your sister?" he asked.

"I'm not sure what's going on with my sister and me, but for now everything is at peace, if that's what you're asking."

"Hey, peaceful is better than being at war, right?" he asked.

"I suppose."

"Listen, I'm loading up a few of these boxes to take to the other office. I plan on spending the rest of the day there sorting out a few odds and ends. I wanted to give you all the time you needed with your sister, but let me know when you're free to talk. We were sort of in the middle of something before she arrived," he said.

"Yeah, sure. We do need to catch up at some point. How about later this evening to at least say goodnight, and maybe sketch out a few plans?"

"Sure," he replied.

Again, he gave her a quick peck, this time on the lips, leaving the scent of fresh mint lingering behind. She watched him roll his hand truck out the door, feeling sorry for the missed time, the interrupted plans, and wishing she could be alone with him once more.

"Ms. Mae, we need to talk," Clara said, abruptly interrupting her second round of coffee.

"Well, good morning to you, too, sweetheart. I have ten minutes before I have to get ready to crank up the boat. What's on your mind?" she asked.

"I overheard part of your conversation with Mike this morning, and I desperately need to know everything Mike shared with you."

Mae carefully placed her mug down on the table.

"No, ma'am. You will not get me caught in the middle of this. Anything you want to know has to come from the source himself."

She continued taking a couple of sips before chucking the rest down the sink, feeling somewhat caught off guard.

"After all I've done to help you and Jonathan when you were at your worst?" Clara asked.

"That's not fair. Nobody asked you for your help. You offered. This is different. Mike confided in me, and I'm not sure how much you heard, but it does no good to go snooping around. Someone is always bound to get hurt while relying upon partial information." Mae argued.

"That's why I'm coming to you. I overheard him say he wants to know more about my life in New York. The least you could do is fill me in on the rest."

"No... no... and more no. Maybe next time you'll think twice before you withhold information from me," Mae said.

"When did I ever withhold information from you?" Clara asked, realizing as soon as the words slipped out of her mouth, Mae was upset that she wasn't included in the conversation with Mackenzie at the café.

"How soon we forget..." Mae replied.

Mae ran into the bathroom like a two-year-old and slammed the door behind her.

"Ms. Mae, seriously?" Clara tried to plea with her on the other side of the door.

"I'd appreciate a little privacy so I can use the restroom in peace, please."

Clara distanced herself, but she didn't go far. As soon as Mae reemerged, she picked up where she left off.

"Ms. Mae, please. It's important to me."

Mae returned to the front, where they could watch for customers.

"Have a seat... relax your nerves for a moment." She directed Clara toward her chair. Once she confirmed the coast was clear, she began speaking.

"I will not repeat what he said verbatim. I'll leave the details up to Mike. However, what I can tell you is he's pretty serious about you. He loves you and wants to be as close as he can to you. I think it concerns him when you're going through something and you don't let him in. You know Mike... he wants to be a part of your world, and he can't do that if you won't communicate with him."

Clara released a sigh.

"My suggestion is whatever you're going through, open up and share it with him." Then, she leaned in closer, giving Clara a directive more so than advice.

"If you love that man, and you want him to be around for the long haul, then you're going to have to get rid of that attitude of yours that believes you can solve all your problems on your own. Open up, Clara. Regardless of how good or bad it is, Mike can handle it."

Clara nodded.

"You're right. I'm just so ashamed of opening up and letting him see all of who I really am. Please, take that the right way... I'm referring to my past more than anything else. A few months back when Keith showed up, I felt so exposed. I didn't ask him to come here, yet everyone in town got a first-hand experience of the dark man from my past. A man that I once referred to as my husband. Now, my sister is here… and man, did she show up with a duffle bag full of drama. I feel like all of it is such a negative reflection on me. What a way to get to know Clara Covington. I feel so embarrassed." She admitted.

"Honey, that's a very tainted point of view. The way I see it… you got rid of the ex and as for family… you can't help who you're related to. Anybody who cares about you will see through that and look at your heart. That's what matters most."

"I guess you're right."

"I know I am. Now, pat your eyes dry and make plans to spend a little time with Mike. Take the day off, head to the beach, plan an evening out… do something. That way the two of you can talk and have some much-needed alone time. As for me, if I don't get my fanny out back, I'm going to be late receiving my customers for my next tour. Next time I see you, I'd like to hear an update." Mae demanded. She was always willing to offer support and a good kick in the pants when needed.

"Yes, ma'am. I'm going to get back to work as well. This office can't run itself," Clara said, patting her eyes and returning to her computer. Before working on her to-do list for the morning, she sent a message to Mike that read *you haven't been gone long and I already miss you. Maybe we could talk tonight in person? Dinner for two on the beach? Love you."*

∿

With a full day of work behind her, Clara laid the ginger ale and crackers down on the counter, listening for movement around the house from Agnes. She glanced over at the sink, filled with dirty dishes, and noticed an assortment of seasonings displayed on the counter and out of place.

"Agnes?"

"I'm downstairs," she yelled faintly from the basement.

Yeah, well, you need to be upstairs cleaning up after yourself, she thought to herself.

She threw her hair up in a bun and went down to check on her.

"The kitchen looks like an absolute disaster area. I hope that means you're better," Clara said.

Agnes laid stretched out over the couch, staring at the evening news.

"Don't lift a fork. I'll get to it as soon as I can find the strength. I don't know what's gotten into me today. I'm feeling a little off today," she said.

"Well, here's your crackers and ginger ale. Whatever you have I sure don't want it. I'm ordering take-out tonight for Mike and me. I'll order something for you as well if you'd like."

"Thanks, but don't worry about me. I'll stay out of sight so you two can enjoy a peaceful evening," she said.

"Okay. Well, holler for me... no, better yet, call my cell if you need me."

"Yeah... about that. They cut my cell service off today. I tried making a call after we spoke, and it wouldn't go through. I guess my pre-paid account needs to be replenished," Agnes said.

Clara stopped talking for a moment, closed her eyes, and silently exhaled.

"You can use the landline if you need to make a call. We'll figure out the rest later on. We'll be down by the beach if you need anything."

She left the basement with mixed feelings of disappointment, and downright aggravation that her sister had now become her dependent. Everything continuously flowed through her mind. But tonight, she was determined to focus on herself and pulling it together for Mike.

As Clara sat next to Mike, in the sand, she considered how to tell him about what was going on. After a meal and nearly an hour passed, she figured the best thing to do was to just come out with it.

"I'm sure you've been wondering what's going on, Mike. I've been mortified to go into the details, but, none of this is my fault, so I'm just going to share. My sister is here because she and Keith broke up and she has nowhere to go," she said.

"Keith? As in your ex? The guy I met a while back?"

"Yes," she said, turning away and looking toward the water.

"What the heck? Wow, that's a lot to digest. Did she explain how this all came about? And, how are you doing with all this? How are you able to cope with her being under the same roof?" he asked.

"It beats me. It's the classic we ran into each other and hit it off kind of story. She says they were desperate... lonely... and from the sound of things, broke. So, basically, they needed each other. That is... until he decided he had enough of her and found a new woman. She showed up at my door with a bruise on her face, Mike. What was I supposed to do?"

"That's a tough situation," he said.

"It sure is. I can hear my mother's voice in the back of my mind, reminding me we share the same blood. Look out for your sister, she would say."

"Even after she didn't talk to you for several years and dated your ex? I have to say, that's loyalty. I don't know that I could do it," he replied.

"Thanks," Clara said in a short tone, grabbing a soda out of the cooler.

"Clara, you know what I mean. I'm frustrated for you, that's all. You've been through enough lately."

She looked at him and relaxed, knowing ultimately that he cared.

"It's like I inherited an added liability, yet she's my sister. I have to figure something out. In the meantime, I just wanted to let you know that I'm trying to be as transparent as possible. It's difficult putting my life on display like this. I left my sister and all the bad portions of my life behind a long time ago, but it's all coming back to haunt me, right here on Solomons Island. Everything is unfolding right before my very eyes," she said.

"Clara, I think you're being a little tough on yourself. Besides, how can we ever get married and live as one if you don't share these kinds of things with me?"

She continued gazing out into the water.

"I'm working on it. Try to put yourself in my shoes for just a minute, Mike. Your life is so squeaky clean. You'd be married today if it wasn't for your fiancé's accident, and you have amazing parents."

"Yeah, amazing parents who just moved to Ft. Lauderdale, and I haven't even been down there to visit yet. You haven't even met them yet... why? Because I'm too busy with my head buried in the sand trying to keep my new business venture up and running. I'm always too busy trying to keep the business afloat... do you think I'm proud to share that side of me?" he asked.

"Okay, so that's an easy fix. We can make plans to

go see your parents. Book a flight... problem solved. My life is a tad bit more complicated."

"This is not your everyday life. Taking her in is a temporary setback. Your life is far better off than your sister's will ever be. All I wanted you to know tonight is that I'm here for you... I'm ready to focus on so much more than just business. I see great things in store for our future."

"So do I," she said.

"I won't lie. This week has shown me there's so much more I need to get to know about you. I want to go to New York and see where you grew up and learn every single little thing about your past. And, I want you to come to Florida and meet my parents, look through albums, and hear stories of what I was like as a kid. But, ultimately... I have a vision for us, Clara. I can see us together for the long haul. It's just a matter of when you'll be free to focus on that vision with me."

"I am free," she whispered.

"Emotionally free, Clara. Take the necessary time to sort things out with your sister first," he said, rubbing her back.

He repositioned himself to sit behind her and massaged her shoulders.

"It's obvious this thing has been weighing you down."

"Mike."

"Yes?"

"Tonight, I want to forget about everything, except for you and me. If only for a little while, let's just lie together under the stars."

"But, what about Agnes?"

"I'll go check on her in a little while. Please. Hold me, Mike."

He laid back on their blanket, opening his arms to make room for her next to him. A huge smile spread across his face as he pointed up toward a shooting star.

"Look, babe. Make a wish," he said.

Clara squeezed her eyes tight and then opened them, kissing him on the cheek.

"Thank you. Did I mention how beautiful you look tonight?" he asked.

"No."

"Well, you do. You look radiant as always." He added.

She brushed her hair off her shoulder.

"Why, thank you, handsome."

Clara returned from the beach to the kitchen to grab a bottle of wine and headed downstairs to briefly check on Agnes. She walked softly, just in case she'd fallen asleep, hoping not to disturb her.

When she reached the bottom of the stairwell to

the basement, she paused, realizing Agnes was on the house phone. She could overhear her conversation.

"Don't you think it's a little too late to be concerned with where I am or who I'm with? I'm so angry with you, I don't know what to do with myself, Keith," she said.

Clara continued listening.

"The only reason I'm calling you is because I can't stop throwing up, and I haven't had my menstrual cycle in over a month. If you thought you had problems before, then you better get ready to face the music if I turn out to be pregnant," Agnes said, speaking in a low and angry tone.

Clara dropped the wine in her hand, causing the glass to shatter everywhere. She immediately dissolved any thoughts of returning to the beach for a romantic evening with Mike.

CHAPTER 6

Clara sped up route four, having flashbacks to the moment she grabbed her wallet and her keys, barely yelling something out to Mike, letting him know she had to leave. With the wind in her hair and the sound of her engine purring, she didn't know where she was going, but she knew she needed an evening drive.

"Oh, come on... not now," she said, banging the steering wheel, noticing the gas gauge was touching on empty.

"Of all the days to forget to fill up the tank. What else could go wrong tonight?"

She pulled into the parking lot of a hardware store where the lights were still on, giving her a small ounce of hope that the place could possibly be open.

She shifted the gear in park, noticing the needle

resting comfortably on E, and the red-light indicator was steady.

"Great. What was I thinking? Single woman runs out of gas after nine p.m. in an empty parking lot without a cell phone. Real smart, Clara, real smart," she said.

She ran to the front door, noticing an older couple and a young teenager arranging items on a shelf.

"Hello," Clara called out, peering through the door, hoping not to startle them.

"Hello there. I'm sorry, we're closed for the evening. I guess one of us forgot to lock the door," the older lady said as she hobbled toward to the front. She was relying on her good foot for the most part.

"Fran, what did I tell you about applying too much pressure on your foot? I can handle the door. You sit down and rest." The older gentleman complained.

"Oh, I'm fine. I can't sit down all day, Jeffrey." She hobbled a little closer.

"We normally close around six. But, tonight we're getting caught up on a few things. What's a pretty lady like yourself doing out here alone... are you lost?"

"No, I'm not lost. I ran out of gas and, unfortunately, I don't have a cell phone to call for help. I'm Clara, by the way," she said, extending her hand.

"Well, Miss Clara, you picked the wrong time of

day to run out of gas. It's so quiet and desolate here in these neck of the woods after a certain hour. You're lucky we stayed later than usual. How far are you away from home?" she asked.

"About forty minutes, give or take. It could've been worse, I guess. I could've ended up next to a farm or corn field out here somewhere. It seems like as soon as you leave the island it's nothing but farm country for several miles," Clara said.

"Yes, my point exactly. You're one lucky lady. I suppose you'll want to use the telephone to call one of your family members to come pick you up?" Fran asked.

Clara wasn't certain who she should call, given that she ran out frantically, leaving Mike stranded and Agnes stunned.

"Yeah," she responded.

"What's the matter, honey? Don't you have anyone to call?"

"Sure. I do, thank you," she said, accepting the phone to dial Mike's number.

The phone rang several times before he picked up.

"Hello."

"Mike..."

"Thank God. Clara, where are you? You ran out of here so fast I didn't have a chance to ask where you were going," he said.

"I know. I needed to clear my head."

74

She noticed Fran standing nearby, taking in every word. Her husband also made his way to the front counter, listening in.

"I hate to do this...but I ran out of gas, and I need a ride back home. Kind of ironic... I guess that's what I get for running off and not paying attention to what I was doing," she said.

"It's not a problem, and you don't have to explain yourself, I completely understand. Your sister told me what happened. It was too much to take in. I get it," he said.

Nobody really gets it until you've walked a mile in my shoes, Clara thought to herself.

"I'm in Huntingtown at the hardware store right off route four."

"Okay, do you feel safe?" he asked.

"Completely. The owners of the store were kind enough to let me come in and use their phone."

"That's good. It's raining here in Solomons, but I'll be there as soon as I can."

"Thank you, Mike," she said, feeling somewhat embarrassed.

"Hey, Clara."

In the background, she could hear him slamming the door and cranking up the engine of his jeep.

"Yes."

"Nevermind. I'm going to stop briefly at a gas station and fill my gas can up with enough to get you up and running again. We'll talk more when we see each other."

"Okay, see you soon."

She hung up, facing a party of three who appeared to be really curious about her.

"Hi, I'm Clara," she said to the gentleman and the teenager who had joined Fran upfront.

"Clara, I'm Jeffrey, and this is our granddaughter, Amelia. It's nice to meet you."

"Jeffrey...Amelia... Fran. Easy names to remember. It's nice to meet you as well. I feel terrible for interrupting your work. I can wait outside in the car. My ride won't be here for a little while," she said.

"We won't hear of it. Pull up a chair and make yourself comfortable. Business was slow today, so it's nice to have someone to talk to outside of ourselves. Isn't that right, Jeffrey?" Fran said.

"Absolutely. Can we offer you something to drink?" he asked.

"Oh, no. I'm fine thank you. The last thing I want to do is be a bother. If I can be of help to you in any way, please let me know. I've never worked in a hardware store, but I'm quick on my feet and I'm a quick study. So, whatever you need just say the word."

"I won't hear of it. You're here as our guest, so go on and make yourself comfortable."

Clara looked around and pulled up a wooden stool. Amelia returned to her responsibilities in aisle two, and Fran remained with her, leaving Jeffrey to fiddle around up front.

"What brings you to Huntingtown at this time of night?" Fran asked.

"I was actually heading north. Just out for an evening drive, really."

"Nowadays, you never can be too safe. Having a cell phone with you is essential. You could've been stranded, having to hitchhike into town. And, honey, trust me, hitchhiking is about one of the worst things an attractive woman like yourself should ever be doing. There are so many crazies out there. Don't you ever watch those night specials that talk about actual crimes happening across the country? I can tell you stories for days about people who went missing then turned up dead or buried in-"

"Fran, is that necessary? You're going to scare the poor woman half to death, for goodness' sake. Even you can't watch those shows without checking the windows and making sure the door is locked." Jeffrey laughed.

"Tell me about it. I'm actually surprised I didn't check the front door tonight before we started working on the inventory. I was preoccupied I suppose."

Fran glanced at Clara's hand, noticing she wasn't wearing a ring.

"Do you have a boyfriend or brother coming to bail you out?" She smiled.

"Yes, my boyfriend is coming. He's used to zipping up and down route four all the time for work. He knows his way around," Clara said.

"Oh, what does he do?"

It was obvious to Clara that Fran was curious by nature, maybe even a tad bit nosey. But, since they were kind enough to take her in on such a dark night, she figured the least she could do was entertain a few questions.

"He owns Lighthouse Tours... not sure if you've heard of it, but they have two locations. One in Solomons and the other up in North Beach. It's nothing for him to drive here. He does it multiple times a week."

"That's nice." She leaned in.

"He must do pretty well for himself if he owns two locations."

Clara smiled to be polite.

"Jeffrey and I have owned this hardware store for what... fifteen years now... isn't that right, sweetheart?"

"Fifteen years and counting," he said.

"Seems like it was just yesterday that we opened up for business. Back then we were crazy enough to invest with my siblings. It was the most chaotic time of our lives. Remember that, Jeffrey? It almost caused us to get a divorce, didn't it, Jeffrey?" She chuckled.

"It sure did. Your brothers were as crazy as they come back then. Especially the oldest one. Thankfully, we survived without having to go out of business. But, I told Fran if she ever comes up with an idea like that again, I would be adios amigos. Needless to say, my wife came to her senses, and fifteen years later we're still happily married, and in business here at the store," he said.

Fran stood beside Jeffrey, patting him on the back.

"He's telling the truth. You know how the saying goes. You can choose your friends, but you can't choose your family." She continued to smile.

Clara found it to be ironic that they would touch on the subject of family. Especially on the heels of everything that was happening in her life.

"So, did you resolve things with your brothers? I'm not sure about the details, but disagreeing over business matters can be rather tough, I would imagine," Clara said.

"That's an understatement. We couldn't seem to get on the same page regarding finances, so that made it even worse. You know how it is when opinions and egos get involved. We thought it would be best to buy them out and salvage the family ties. Don't get me wrong, I was ready to kick them to the curb, but I'd never forgive myself if Fran had to sever ties with her own flesh and blood. It wasn't worth it. Thankfully, we worked everything out... and now, as they say, everything else is history." Jeffrey explained.

Fran wore more of a serious expression on her face.

"Don't mind us. If you sit here long enough, we can tell you stories for days. Enough about me and my siblings. What about you? Do you have a lot of family here in Maryland?" she asked.

"No, I don't. I have a sister who's in town visiting, but we're from New York. I moved here several years ago. I love living by the water and don't see myself leaving anytime soon."

"Well, that's nice," Fran replied.

"It's funny you should mention not getting along with your sibling. My sister and I have struggled with being on the same page for most of our lives," Clara said, looking downward.

"Honey, welcome to the club. I've never seen three people born from the same woman, with such vastly distinct personalities. I mean so different until it used to make me wonder if some of us were adopted." She laughed.

"I'm teasing, of course. Family is all you have. So, we'll continue to do as we've always done... learn to forgive, try to forget, and move on with life." Fran continued.

"But, what if you can't forgive anymore? What if you've simply reached the end of your rope?"

Fran came from behind the counter.

"Something tells me you're currently going through something," Fran said.

"Yes, except the only difference is it appears to be a lifelong thing for me. Not just an incident here and there. My sister and I have always been at odds." Clara shrugged her shoulders.

"You and your husband have been so gracious to let me hang out here until my ride shows up. The last thing you need is a stranger unloading all of her problems on you." She continued.

Fran hobbled a few feet away, reaching for another stool and made herself comfortable.

"I'm a big believer in the idea that things happen for a reason. It's no coincidence that your gas ran out here. It could've happened anywhere... but perhaps I have something in my arsenal of tools that I can impart to help you with your situation. So, unload if you want to. Tell me what's on your mind. Maybe I can help," she said, folding her arms, ready to listen.

"Eh, there's so much I wouldn't know where to begin," Clara responded, wondering how far she should go with a stranger.

"Honey, I have two siblings that almost caused us to lose this business. One who still causes trouble every year when he shows up for family holidays, and the other whose finances are so out of sorts he's practically become a child of mine. Would you like for me to go on?" She smiled.

Clara relaxed a bit.

"No, it's okay. It's obvious you understand where I'm coming from. Of course, the details may differ a bit, but I guess we all have challenges, don't we?" she said.

"Exactly."

"Well, as I mentioned, in my situation, my sister and I grew up at odds. She was always the ungrateful and self-centered one, always looking to get over. Have you ever met somebody who depletes and drains the life out of you by the choices they make?" she asked.

"Certainly. We all have I would imagine."

"Yeah, well, that's my sister. Except I thought I freed myself from that over ten years ago when I left New York. Now, she's back... and the only reason is because she's in trouble and desperately needs help. You mentioned having a dependent, and I know exactly what that's like. The worst part is I finally have a life now. I spent several years focusing on work, and I've finally come out of my shell and met an amazing man. But, just when life was going really good, she shows up," Clara said, sounding weaker the more she spoke.

"Sweetheart, listen to me. You're probably not going to want to hear this, but the worst thing you could ever do is run from your problems. You've got to embrace this head-on. Confront things with your sister, set your expectations, and always believe there's room for healing."

"I'm not running," Clara responded.

Fran tilted her head downward, being intentional about looking Clara in the eye.

"I don't know you that well, but in this brief conversation, you've shared enough details to let me know you're running. What do you call leaving your home state of New York? Or better yet, getting in your car tonight and fleeing whatever transpired back home?"

Clara adjusted herself upright, sitting at full attention. Fran's words of wisdom stung and left her feeling exposed.

"Even if that's the case, she pushed it way too far this time. There's no turning back. Eh eh... no way. At this point I'm starting to think I'm better off when I stay disconnected from everyone... that way my life can be free of disappointment, embarrassment, and the shame that comes along with having to share this with others. It's too much." She confessed.

Fran tapped her pointer finger on the counter, not holding back an ounce of passion.

"I don't know what she did or didn't do, but none of it is worth losing close relationships over. Those who truly love you will understand. You have to trust and believe it's true," she said.

Jeffrey returned from his work, pointing toward the front door.

"Ladies, I hate to interrupt your conversation, but it appears as though a vehicle has pulled up in the parking lot. I thought it might be your ride," he said.

Shortly after, a car door slammed, the door opened, and Mike stepped in waving at Clara. Fran took one last opportunity to conclude their conversation.

"Try not to close yourself off to others when things get tough. I'm older than you and already had to learn these lessons the hard way. The only one who will truly suffer in the end is you."

Mike walked up to Clara, giving her a kiss and placing her cell phone in her hands.

"I made it here as quickly as I could. Are you okay?" he asked.

"I'm fine. Fran and Jeffrey have been gracious hosts. I don't know what I would've done without them."

"It was our pleasure to have you. This was a pleasant end to the workday. I'm just sorry we couldn't talk longer," Fran said.

She then turned to address Mike.

"Be sure to keep a close eye on her. She's quite the gem," she said, smiling.

"I certainly will, ma'am," Mike responded, extending his hand.

"Please, call me Fran."

"All right, Fran."

Clara shared one last heartfelt word of gratitude and invited them down to Solomons sometime.

"If you 're ever in the area, we'd love to have you down for a tour," she said, and Mike concurred.

"That's a great idea. Please, as my way of saying thank you, it's on the house. Come anytime." He offered.

Jeffrey and Fran thanked them and waited by the front door until Clara's car was up and running.

~

Her cell phone rang as she followed Mike down route four. The screen flashed Mike's name. She knew in the pit of her stomach he would have questions, and she would have some explaining to do.

"Hi," she answered.

"How are you doing back there?"

"I'm fine. I didn't realize it was going to down-pour like this tonight. It's awful out here."

"I know. To think you would've been on the road in this weather by yourself even if you didn't run out of gas is pretty scary," he said.

"I know. It was stupid of me to take off like that. I should've at least slowed down for a second to grab my phone."

"No, Clara. A better solution may have been to run out and talk with me. Or if you didn't want to talk, at least sit with me, so I would know that you're okay. You don't deserve your sister showing up in your life and dropping all this on your plate, I get it. But, the people in your life who love and care about you don't deserve to be worried sick about you all the time. Honestly, I don't get why your only response is to run. You have more of a say so in this than you think," he said, trying to plea on her behalf.

"Mike, that's well said, coming from an outsider looking in. But, it's not as easy as you're making it sound," she replied.

There was a moment of silence, followed by the sound of heavy rain and windshield wipers on both ends of the line.

"So, I'm an outsider now?" he asked.

"Mike, you know what I mean. I'm going through a lot right now, and I don't have the patience for your overly sensitive feelings about every little thing." She retorted.

"Mmm, I see. Well, on that note, you know best. Me and my sensitive feelings will stay out of it."

Clara's eyes burned with aggravation, mixed with regret for not choosing her words more carefully. She refrained from saying another word, creating an awkward ending to their conversation and car ride home.

CHAPTER 7

$\mathcal{M}$ ackenzie closed the cash register in time to look up and see Brody walking in. He removed his baseball cap, nodding his head to greet a customer before looking her way.

"Brody, is that you?" she asked.

His face lit up with a smile.

"Yep, it's me... in the flesh. Figured I'd come over and try something from your menu before I start working on the boats this afternoon," he replied.

"I can't remember the last time I've seen you in here. I always thought you were more of a bring your lunch from home kind of guy. I think you used to tell me it was your way of saving money for a rainy day, isn't that right?" she asked, grabbing a menu and leading him to a window seat.

The afternoon bridge club gathered in the center

of the café, reshuffling their cards, and taking restroom breaks before the next round.

Brody took a seat at a booth.

"Technically, that's true. I try to be wise with my
funds, however I've been told more than once that I
need to learn to get out more. So, I figured I'd start by
coming over here and treating myself to a nice
lunch," he said, clearing his throat and adjusting his
clothing.

"Okay. Sounds good to me. You look nice, by the
way. You certainly don't present yourself like a man
who works with dirty motors and parts all day."

"Thank you." He smiled at her, probably a
minute longer than he should've, but he found her to
be attractive and couldn't help but stare.

"Today for our specials we have a delicious corn
chowder soup, red snapper, or a hot brisket sandwich
if you're interested."

"It all sounds delicious. Now I see why the others
like to come over here so much," he said, skimming
over the menu.

"We definitely should have something to satisfy
your palate. I'll tell you what. Take a few minutes to
glance over the menu and I'll be right back to take
your order. Can I grab something to drink for you?"
she asked.

"A glass of water will do."

Again, he looked her in the eyes and smiled, this

time quickly returning to the menu as not to look like a weirdo.

Mackenzie passed by the bridge club table, checking to see if anyone needed refills on their drinks.

"Ms. Violet, is your tea still nice and hot? I can bring some more hot water if you'd like?"

"I'm good. Thank you, Mackenzie. It's time for me to kick some serious butt in this next round. If anybody tries to stop my winning streak, they're going down," she said, pumping her fists in the air.

"Oh, dear. All right, I'll leave you to it." Mackenzie laughed.

"By the way, I'd like you to meet the newest member of the club. Darla, this is Mackenzie... she's the head boss in charge... tip her well and she'll take good care of you. Isn't that right, Mackenzie?"

"Ms. Violet, I'd like to believe you get stellar service from me whether a tip is included or not." She smiled.

"Hey, I'm just trying to look out for you, that's all," Ms. Violet said.

"Mackenzie, it's nice to finally meet you. I'm new to the area, but I've already been hearing rave reviews about the café. Trust me, I don't like to cook much, so don't be surprised if you see me in here every day."

"Well, we're happy to serve you, Ms. Darla."

"Please, call me Darla. Ms. Darla makes me

sound old. In my mind, I'm not a day over forty." She chuckled.

Ms. Violet found her comment to be humorous.

"You ought to stop telling yourself those lies," she said, glancing over her cards.

It was all Mackenzie could do to keep a straight face in front of these women.

"I'm teasing. You look dashing, honey. Why don't you go ahead and try a slice of that hot apple pie you ordered before it cools down? I want to whisper something to Mackenzie right quick," she said, motioning for Mackenzie to come closer.

"Is everything okay?" Mackenzie asked, lowering her voice.

"Oh, yes. Everything is fine. But, I noticed that fella over there... the one you seated by the window. He's been staring at you from the moment he walked in to the moment you walked over here. I think has a little crush on you." Violet winked.

"Oh no, Ms. Violet. He's one of the guys from Lighthouse Tours across the street. There's nothing there." She chuckled, dismissing the idea immediately.

"Listen. I might be seventy-seven, but I still have twenty-twenty vision. What I just saw was a man admiring you from afar. You don't have to pay attention to me if you don't want to, but last I heard, you are single and on the market. I wouldn't be so dismissive if I were you," Violet said, bluntly, no different than a grandmother without a filter.

"Ms. Violet!" Mackenzie smiled.

"Don't Ms. Violet me. I call it as I see it. Now, let me get back to my bridge game so I can show these folks how the game is supposed to be played."

Mackenzie walked away, shaking her head and still somewhat laughing at the ridiculous idea. Behind the counter, she grabbed a glass, filled it with ice, and continued mumbling about Ms. Violet.

"What are you over here talking to yourself about? Did somebody ruffle your feathers?" Josh asked.

"Not hardly. Just receiving my daily dose of entertainment from the bridge club, that's all."

"That explains everything. You never know what they're capable of saying or doing from one day to the next," he replied, while mopping the floor.

"Exactly."

Mackenzie looked over at Brody, who appeared to still be mulling over the menu.

"Hey, Josh."

"Hmm?"

"By any chance, has Bill been by the café on my days off? I was wondering if you met his new lady yet?"

"Sorry, kiddo. You know I would tell you if I knew anything, but it's almost as if Bill disappeared into thin air. I haven't even seen him around town. It's pretty strange if you ask me."

"Hmm, interesting. Oh, well. Let me bring Brody his water and see what he wants to eat. I'll be right back. Oh, and Josh, keep that between the two of us, okay?" she yelled over her shoulder.

"Secret is safe with me." He continued to mop.

Mackenzie wanted to forget Bill existed but couldn't help but wonder how she would react the next time he showed up at the café, particularly with another woman on his arm. In some ways, she felt kind of dumb, assuming he would ever return. *Maybe he was too embarrassed to step foot in the café,* she thought.

"Okay, what will it be? Would you like one of our specials or something from the menu?"

Brody closed the menu and laid it down.

"I'll give the chowder a try for now."

"That's it? Are you going to make it through the rest of the day on a bowl of corn chowder?" she asked.

"I'll tell you what... throw in a roll to go with it. Maybe even a date for two this weekend, and I think I'll be just fine."

Mackenzie wrote down the corn chowder on her notepad, but froze after mistakenly writing the word date. She scratched the word out and looked up at him.

"What was that again?" she asked.

Brody's face turned bright red. Instant regret settled in the pit of his stomach. He knew he should've waited to hear from Clara, rather than make such a bold move.

"You mean the part about the date? Yeah, that was my ridiculous way of trying to ask you out. Look, I'm sorry. I'm not good at this sort of thing. It's just... I heard you weren't seeing anybody, and I've always thought you were beautiful with a real friendly personality, so I figured I'd gather up the courage to come in here and ask you out. Stupid move on my part, I know. It will never happen again," he said, looking off in another direction in total shame and embarrassment.

Mackenzie noticed his side profile, his fresh haircut, and how neatly put together he was. She assumed he made the extra effort for her but wasn't sure.

"I'm sorry, Brody."

"No... no... it's okay. It's probably best I take the chowder to go. I can't sit here and eat after making such a fool of myself. It will probably be another six months before I can walk in here without feeling like a complete idiot," he said, laughing it off.

"I mean... I'm sorry. I misunderstood what you were saying at first. My answer is yes," she said, figuring maybe this would be a nice distraction.

He slowly raised his head to make sure he was following correctly.

"Wait... what?"

"Yes. I'll go on a date with you. A date for two this weekend sounds nice. I could stand to get out more, myself," she said.

A huge smile appeared on his face. He passed the menu along, placing it in her hands, trying not to reveal too much enthusiasm.

"Why, thank you. I believe you just made me the happiest man on Solomons Island," he said, with both of them letting out a little laughter.

"Can I pick you up at your place on Saturday around four?" he asked, slightly exposing his dimples.

"I have to secure a sitter for my daughter, but that shouldn't be a problem. Four should work fine. Let me head to the back and grab your chowder. I'll be right back," she said, walking away, biting her lower lip to contain herself.

"Hey, Mack," he called out.

She turned around.

"Do you enjoy hanging out by the water?" he asked.

"Are you kidding me? We live on Solomons Island. Who doesn't like hanging out by the water? I'll write my address down on a napkin when I get back." She smiled and continued heading toward the kitchen, intentionally winking at Ms. Violet.

~

Jonathan sat next to Mae on the front porch with a laptop in hand, showing her pictures of various boats to buy. He felt like a kid in a candy shop, bubbling over and excited about potentially purchasing his dream toy.

"Look at this one. It's a forty-seven-footer with plenty of space for us to invite family and friends whenever we want to take a trip," he said.

"Whoa, she's nice looking but rather large, don't you think?"

"Well, of course, we'd have to consider what marina we'd like to use. But, I'm certain they'll have options for different size boat slips. It shouldn't be an issue."

"Jonathan, would you look at the price tag on that boat? You have to be kidding me. We don't have that kind of money," Mae said, frowning.

"Boats aren't cheap, but don't worry. I have a few extra dollars put away. How about this one, instead?"

Mae positioned herself to comfortably scroll through a few of the photos.

"I think this one looks more like my cup of tea," she replied, pointing to a smaller version, approximately half the size of what Jonathan picked out.

He began relaxing his posture on the back of his chair.

"If we're really looking at this as an opportunity to have a second home we can travel in, I think we ought to do it right the first time. Let's purchase something we can comfortably enjoy," Jonathan said.

"I can comfortably enjoy a trip on any of these options I just showed you. Isn't there a way we can find a boat that won't hurt the bank account? I know you have funds saved up, but this was supposed to be a joint venture. Something we can both contribute to and make our own."

"Mae, I'm all for us making it our own. When you first presented the idea, you really leaned in heavy on me fulfilling my dreams. I'm not dreaming of a miniature sailboat that requires me to squeeze in like a can of sardines at night when I want to lie next to my wife." He grumbled.

She passed him the laptop and reached for her water can instead.

"When I presented the idea, I also had no intentions of purchasing a boat the size of Taj Mahal. Let's be reasonable here. We are two tour guides, living in a quaint little cottage who are both closer to retirement more than anything else. Just because we have the money saved up doesn't mean it's wise to spend it," she said.

"What are you so afraid of?" Jonathan asked, but regretted the words as soon as they slipped out, knowing it would probably spark another one of their newlywed spats.

"I'm not afraid of anything. Jonathan Middleton... before this conversation gets way out of hand,

I'm going to water my flowers. Perhaps it's best for us to table this for now and set aside a day to see the boats in person."

"Fine."

"Fine." She repeated and walked off to tend to her garden.

Jonathan shut down his computer and looked up to the sight of Meredith, the next-door neighbor, staring in his direction... more like eavesdropping if he was being honest. She was single, president of the HOA, ran regular meetings for the neighborhood and had a reputation for being the town mayor, or the most inquisitive person in the neighborhood.

"How are you, Meredith?" He waved, wishing he was already inside.

"I'm fantastic, Jonathan. Couldn't be better. How are you and Mae coming along?"

"We're doing well. Trying to enjoy a little fresh air before it's time to head in for the evening."

"That's nice. In the market for a boat, I see," she said, eagerly waiting for him to share more information.

"Yep, something like it."

"Sounds fun. We used to go sailing every now and again when I was growing up. I miss it. It's part of the reason I moved out here to Solomons... not to sail, but to be near the water and all." She smiled.

"Yes, the water is a big attraction."

She gripped her hands around a warm beverage, took a sip, and continued probing.

"So, you're thinking about living on a boat and traveling... would you consider selling your property?" she asked.

Mae reappeared in time to catch Meredith in the middle of her inquisitiveness.

"Well, there she is. Meredith, I haven't seen you in a couple of days. I was wondering why you haven't been at your post keeping up with what's going on in the neighborhood," Mae said, smirking at her.

Meredith hopped up and gathered her beverage and a few other items.

"Haha, Mae. I know what you're trying to imply, but it's okay. I was just about to go inside. I hope you two can settle your differences. Oh, and a small piece of advice before I go... you might consider closing your bedroom window this evening, so the rest of us don't have to overhear one for your nightly escapades," she said. She stuck her tongue out at Mae and slammed the front door behind her.

The two had sort of a funny love-hate relationship. Occasionally, they stopped the constant banter to unite on a common cause, but for the most part, this was their norm.

"You carry on like two old grumpy sisters, constantly taking jabs at one another," Jonathan said.

Mae waved her hand dismissively.

"We've been neighbors for so long I don't pay it

any mind. I just get a kick out of letting her know how nosey I think she is, that's all," she said.

Jonathan shook his head and laughed. At least Meredith helped to break the tension between them.

"Come over here, Mae. Did you have a chance to cool down while you were watering your flowers? Your watering session was short-lived, I noticed," he said.

She climbed the front steps and returned to her rocking chair.

"Yes, I'm fine. How about yourself?"

"Hey, I'm fine with whatever the eventual out-come is. What's most important is that I have you to experience life's adventures with. All the rest really isn't that important in the grand scheme of things. I'm sorry I started getting so bent out of shape. It won't happen again," he responded.

"Are you sure about that? I highly doubt that's the last time we'll disagree about something."

"You have a point there, but for now there's at least one thing we can agree on," he said.

"What's that?"

"Leaving the window wide open tonight to annoy the heck out of Meredith."

"I heard that!" Meredith yelled from the window off her front porch.

Jonathan and Mae glanced at each other and laughed so hard they could barely contain themselves.

CHAPTER 8

Clara threw a frisbee to Holly and then sank her toes into the sand, preparing for her morning quiet time. She didn't have to be at work for a couple of hours and decided to start the day in her favorite place for morning meditation.

Her first thought was of Mike and how she hadn't spoken to him since his departure, when she was interrupted.

"Clara, do you have a few minutes to talk?" Agnes asked.

"I didn't hear you coming," she said, straightening up, directing most of her attention to Holly.

"Yeah, I didn't want to disturb you, but I figured since we didn't talk last night..."

Agnes waited for an open invitation to continue.

"There's not much to say, Agnes. I heard enough

when I came down to check and make sure you were okay last night."

"Right. About that... You deserve to know so much more than what you overheard."

"Deserve?" Clara laughed.

"Interesting choice of words. I'm not sure about what I deserve, but I can tell you what I don't deserve."

Agnes joined her, creating a space to sit down.

"Okay, let it out. If this is what it takes to get us talking, let me have it," she responded.

Clara threw the frisbee again, avoiding eye contact with Agnes.

"I don't deserve you showing up unannounced after ten years, expecting me to help pick up the pieces of your broken life," she said.

"Okay, I expected that one. What else do you have for me?"

Clara looked annoyed, causing Agnes to stop talking and just listen to what she had to say.

"I also don't deserve you inadvertently bringing Keith back into my life again. I was in the clear, the divorce was settled, and I had moved on with my life. But, in a lot of ways, I'm not surprised. It's no different than when we were young. You were never content with having your own and never satisfied unless you were causing someone else heartache," Clara said.

"Ouch. That's a bit below the belt. Is that really what you think of me?"

"Yes, it is. I would never say such a thing if it wasn't true. Do you realize the last time we were together we were arguing over mom and dad's benefits after their accident? That should've been a time of healing... a time for us to come together and be there for one another, but sadly, we couldn't. Now, years later, I'm still trying to figure out why you never reached out to see how I was doing or to make amends. One would think after all this time we would've forgiven each other and moved on... but no... we can't because now we're consumed with Keith and your secret baby," she said.

Clara was so disgusted she could feel her blood boiling. She was granted a rare opportunity to speak her mind, and she didn't plan on holding anything back.

"I can hear the gossip now. *Clara's sister was dating her ex and now she's having a baby with him.* Oh boy, I'll never be able to show my face around here after this gets out," she said.

"Wow. I'm sorry I'm such an embarrassment to you."

Clara squinted in total disbelief, then stood up and dusted herself off.

"Don't do that. It's not fair for you to turn this around on me. You do not realize what it's like to be in my shoes. You showed up for selfish reasons,

Agnes. You're not here because you care. Meanwhile, I'm in love with the man of my dreams, but I guess I'm supposed to put all that on hold to cater to you. Well, I'm sorry, but Keith... the baby... all this is too much. You need to figure out a way to let him help you because I can't, Ag. This is way too messy. You need to leave."

Clara whistled for Holly to follow her back to the house, leaving Agnes on the beach alone.

At Lighthouse Tours, Tommy pulled out of the dock with his first tour of the day. Jonathan was close behind him, welcoming the last customer on his boat and preparing to set sail.

Inside, Clara worked on a few marketing ideas when the phone rang.

"Lighthouse Tours, how may I help you?" she answered.

"Hi, Clara, it's Mike."

"Oh, hey. I wasn't looking at the screen before I picked up. How are you this morning?" she asked.

"I'm well. Just calling to run down a list of things that need to get done this week if you have a moment."

She cleared her throat.

"Sure, you sound so formal. Is everything okay?"

"Couldn't be better. I have a lot to get done and

since I'm going to be at the North Beach office for the next couple of weeks, I figured it would be best if I delegate a few of the tasks, that's all."

Clara felt uneasy about Mike's tone but grabbed a pen so she could be ready.

"A couple of weeks? That's unusual for you."

"Yeah, there are a few big-ticket items that need my attention here. Plus, I could use a break from driving back and forth between the two locations. You guys will be fine. The Solomons office is running like a well-oiled machine," he responded.

He became silent on the other end of the line.

"Mike, before you get started, I want to apologize for being short with you the other night. I think we should set aside some time to talk again if it's all right with you."

"It's okay. Really. I understand. I think it's best that you focus on your sister. I'm sure she really needs you right now," he said, getting to the point.

He redirected the conversation, spouting off a list of important items to tackle, remaining professional, and then concluded the call.

"Great, Clara. That conversation was successful," she said out loud to herself after hanging up the phone.

Mae walked in the front door, dusting the bottom of her shoes on the doormat.

"Good morning, Darlin. What are you frowning about so early in the morning?"

"Oh, Ms. Mae. There isn't enough time to get into it. Mike's working out of the North Beach office for the next two weeks... and oh, before I forget, it looks like your tour for this morning was canceled. Sorry, I didn't catch you soon enough to tell you before you left the house."

Mae placed her things down on the back counter.

"I hope this isn't a sign of what's coming. This is literally the third cancellation in the last two weeks. Do you think folks are getting tired of my tours?" she asked.

"No, not at all. I think it's a sign that the weather is shifting, and people are focusing on more indoor activities, that's all. I keep telling Mike that we need to revamp things for the winter months to try to drum up some new business, but I guess he's focused on so many other things."

"Well, that's okay. I ought to be used to it by now. Every business has a busy and a slow season, right?"

"I suppose," Clara responded.

"Did you have a chance to talk things over with Mike?"

"Yes and no."

"Which is it?" Mae asked.

"We barely scratched the surface. Things didn't go the way I hoped they would and now I think he's distancing himself. It's to be expected. All I've focused on these last few days is my sister who couldn't care less about me."

"Oh, I wouldn't go that far."

"That's because you don't know my sister," Clara grunted.

Just then, Mackenzie walked in with a couple of brown paper bags in hand that smelled like fresh bagels. The sight of her dear friend warmed Clara's heart.

"Clara Covington, where have you been?" she asked, laying down the bags and giving Clara and Ms. Mae a hug.

"I know. I'm guilty as charged. I promise I haven't been hiding from you," she said.

Mae chimed in, looking forward to the girl time just as much as Clara.

"Perfect timing. Clara was about to update me on how things were going with her sister. Grab a chair and make yourself comfortable. Hopefully, you brought enough bagels for the rest of us?" Mae said.

"Yes, Ms. Mae, you know I wouldn't forget about you," Mackenzie said, smiling.

Mae pulled a few paper plates out of the cabinet. She figured since she was free, why not pull up a chair and indulge in breakfast and friendly conversation for a little while.

"I came over to check on my girl here and make sure everything is okay. The café hasn't been the same without you, love," Mackenzie said.

"Thanks, Mack. Trust me. I'm trying so hard to get back to normal as soon as I can. I asked Agnes to make plans to go elsewhere this morning. I've had all that I can take."

"How did she respond?"

Clara could feel herself getting worked up all over again.

"I don't know. I walked away without waiting for feedback. What was I supposed to do? She showed up out of nowhere and has literally turned my world upside down."

Mae stopped spreading her grape jam long enough to inquire further.

"Well, what on earth did she do that was so terrible?"

"Let's see. For starters, she dated my ex-husband and is now pregnant with his baby. I just found the last part out by accidentally walking in and over-hearing a conversation she was having with Keith. Need I say more?" she asked.

"No. That about sums it up. Now it makes sense why you're ready to kick her to the curb," Mae replied.

Mackenzie hugged Clara again before pulling up a chair.

"This has been one heck of a year for you. Can we have some good news... You know, a string of good luck for a change. Something positive for goodness' sake," Mackenzie said.

"I'm with you, Mack. I need more than good luck at this point. I need a miracle. I took Ms. Mae's advice and had an honest talk with Mike, only to have that backfire before the evening was over. You guys don't know how much I messed things up."

"What happened?" Mackenzie asked.

"The quick version... I walked downstairs to check on Agnes because she wasn't feeling well. That's when I overheard her talking to Keith. Next thing I know, I was grabbing my keys and storming out the house, leaving Mike sitting on the beach by himself," Clara said.

"Oh, no," Mae replied.

"It gets worse. I ran out of gas by the time I reached Huntingtown, and I didn't have my cell phone. Thankfully, this sweet couple took me in and let me use the phone in their hardware store."

"That was kind," Mack said.

"It was. Fran, the store owner, sat and talked with me for a while. It turns out we actually have a lot in common. But, once Mike got there, and we could gas up and drive back... I don't know... the conversation went south pretty quickly. If I had to do it all over again, I'd take back what I said... or at least do a better job of explaining, but with my head so caught up in my sister's drama, I can't focus on giving him my all right now. I want to, but-"

"You're distracted. It's to be understood." Mae added.

"Try telling that to Mike. I don't think he sees things from the same point of view. Hence, the reason I believe he's distancing himself and working in North Beach for the next couple of weeks." Clara explained.

Mae took a bite out of her bagel, holding her finger up to explain.

"Don't worry about him. He'll come around. The one thing I can tell you from our conversation is it's obvious he loves you. Don't lose sight of that."

"Thanks for the reminder. This morning's conversation was so cold and to the point."

"Ms. Mae is right. He'll come around. Maybe you can take a night off from dealing with your sister and go over to his place and remind him how much he's needed in your life," Mackenzie said.

"That's a good idea."

"In the meantime, what do you plan to do about your sister? Personally, I'd be ready to knock my sister into next week if I ever found out she was sleeping with one of my exes. Even if the relationship was over, it's the principle behind the whole thing," Mae said.

"Thank you! My point, exactly. I feel like she ripped open a fresh wound. I just closed that chapter and although there are no more personal ties, why would she ever decide to fall for Keith? Of all guys... really?" Clara said.

"All right, before we get all riled up, let's put

things in proper perspective. Is she wrong? Yes, absolutely. But, she doesn't have a place to go according to what you told me, Clara. Are you really going to kick her out?"

"Heck, yeah, she should kick her out!" Mae said with a little too much enthusiasm.

Mackenzie and Clara stared at her.

"Oh, I'm sorry. Carry on," Mae responded.

Clara stopped to take a phone call from a customer. She busied herself jotting a few items down, then conducted a little research on the computer before concluding the call.

"Okay, where was I?" she asked.

"You were about to describe your plans for kicking Agnes to the curb," Mae said with a smirk on her face.

Clara looked to the ceiling, stretching back in her chair.

"Do you remember the stories I used to tell about how my former boss Joan and I bonded so well?"

Mae and Mackenzie nodded. "Sure, we do. You used to talk about her all the time," Mack replied.

"She was there for me when I first moved to Solomons Island. We had a lot of wonderful things in common and we were both a support system for one another. I was more than just her housekeeper. We were both stranded by family members who lived self-centered lives."

"Yes, and I'm sure her reasons were justified for

doing so, but you're not Joan. The real question is what does Clara want to do? The Clara I know may be hurt, but she would never go against her parents' wishes and cut off all ties with her sister. You would at least see that she has somewhere to go, Clara," Mackenzie said.

"Hmm," Mae grunted.

"I told her she should stay with Keith. This is his responsibility, don't you think?" Clara asked.

"You mean, Keith, the same guy who already moved on to another woman? Yeah, that sounds like a solid plan," Mack said.

"Hey, wait a minute. Whose side are you on?" Clara asked.

"I'm not taking sides. But, I know you well enough to challenge your thinking about what you're doing. I'm not saying she has to live with you, but it's been ten long years and she's the only family you have, Clara."

"No. You guys are my only family. You, Ms. Mae, the entire lighthouse staff have been more like family to me than Agnes will ever be," she said, with her eyebrows folded like an accordion.

"I know, sweetheart, but whether you like it or not, you and Agnes share the same blood. Nobody ever said forgiveness was easy. But, it may be your only option if you want to hold on to the last family member with a bloodline that connects to your parents." Mackenzie suggested.

A cloud of grief hung over Clara.

"Okay, let's switch things up a bit to lighten the mood," Mackenzie said.

"Great idea," Clara responded.

Mackenzie leaned in closer, lowering her voice.

"Is Brody here?" she asked.

"No, he's in North Beach with Mike," Mae responded.

"Okay, good. Y'all will never believe this, but guess who asked me to go on a date the other day?" McKenzie asked.

"Uhh. Let me take a guess... could it be... Brody?" Mae said, kidding around with her.

"Did you know about this? I had no idea he was interested in going out with me."

"You can blame me for that. He approached me, asking about your dating status, and I told him I'd look into it. But, I've been so consumed that it sort of slipped my mind," Clara said.

"I'm a big believer in all things happening for a reason. Don't worry about it," Mackenzie replied.

"Wait. What's going on with you and Bill? Did the two of you call it quits?" Clara asked.

"He called it quits on me. Turns out he met another woman on the job, and I guess she possessed more of the qualities he was looking for in a woman."

"I know what she possessed, all right." Mae chuckled.

Mackenzie and Clara cracked a smile but investigated little to find out what Mae meant by it. Mainly because they feared whatever crazy comments might follow.

"Whatever the case may be with the new woman, I'm over it. I'll admit my insecurities were getting the best of me at first. I asked Josh if he'd seen Bill and his new woman around, but he hadn't. Then, I started thinking to myself, why do I even care? As for Brody, I'm not sure if anything will come of it, but he is good-looking, kind, and his timing couldn't be better because I need a pleasant distraction right about now."

"I can actually see the two of you together. Just make sure he doesn't become your rebound guy. It took a lot of courage for him to speak up. I'd hate to see him get hurt," Clara said.

"Clara, you know me better than that. The way he came in and ordered something so he could talk to me was sweet. Ms. Violet saw it coming all the way from across the room. He was so nervous he almost got up and left. I wouldn't dare experiment with his feelings," she said.

"Where are you going on your hot date?" Mae asked.

"I'm not sure. All I know is he's picking me up around four this Saturday, and he asked me if I like the water."

"This ought to be interesting. I can't imagine Brody being the romantic type. All he ever does is work and head home for the evening." Mae continued.

"Apparently, that's not all he has up his sleeve. I think he's really into you, Mack," Clara said.

The three looked at each other with smiles at the prospect of budding love. Only time would tell if Brody and Mackenzie would hit it off, or if they would be nothing more than good friends.

CHAPTER 9

"Agnes, are you downstairs?" Clara peeked into the basement but saw nothing, except for a few bags.

"Agnes?" She searched on the main floor, almost giving up when she caught a glimpse of her standing on the deck.

She rolled the sliding glass door open and stepped outside.

"I've been looking for you," Clara said.

"I was hoping to catch you as well. I have everything packed up and I promise I'll be on my way soon. I just wanted to talk to you one last time. I know I haven't been the best sister in the world, but please hear me out, Clara." She begged.

Clara sat in a nearby chair.

"We probably both have a lot to say, but you can go first." She offered.

"I'm not pregnant."

"How can you be so sure?" Clara asked, feeling a rush of relief.

"Right after you left this morning, I drove to the local pharmacy and picked up a test. The minus sign showed up very clear... you can't miss it. I saved it in case you wanted to see it for yourself."

"But, what about the conversation I overheard you having with Keith?" Clara asked.

Agnes felt like she was at a loss for words.

"My cycle was late, and I hadn't been feeling well for a couple of days, so I just assumed it had to mean that I was pregnant. This morning I was planning to tell you about my plans to take the test, but our conversation didn't exactly go as planned."

Clara closed her eyelids.

"I'm not sure what you're expecting from me as your sister, but you have to know this isn't easy for me," she said.

"I know, and I am so sorry. Really, Clara. There's nothing I can say to fix the mess that I've created, but the least I can do is show you. I never intended to show up and ruin your life like this. I always hoped we'd reconnect on better terms."

Clara leaned back in her chair, not knowing whether to feel relieved or to brace herself for the next wave of turmoil.

"I'm sincere when I say I don't want to be a burden to you any more than I already have. It's my hope that although we reunited under terrible circumstances, we can still have a fresh start and be close to one another like mom and dad always wanted. If that's out of the question, then I've already packed my bags. I'll leave today. All you have to do is say the word." Agnes offered, holding her breath, waiting to hear from Clara.

"Where are you going to live?"

"Out of my car if I have to. I've been in worse situations. I'm a New Yorker, remember. I can handle it," she said.

"Are you out of your mind?" You can't live out of a car with nothing but a designer bag and no cell phone service. You wouldn't last one day, and you know it," Clara said, laughing at her.

When the laughter simmered down, Clara's curiosity got the best of her.

"Did you tell Keith?" she asked.

"Not yet."

"Good. Wait, a while longer. Make him sweat a little," Clara said.

Agnes chuckled.

"I'm not kidding. He deserves to sweat from all the pain he's caused. Were you aware that he came to my house a few months back, threatening me for a portion of my inheritance?" she asked.

"No. According to him, he hasn't seen you in

years. I just went along with his story, not really thinking much of it because I also hadn't seen you in a long time."

Clara looked at her suspiciously.

"Believe me. I knew nothing about your inheritance, and I certainly didn't know Keith was in touch with you. What a scumbag," Agnes said.

"He's a scumbag, all right."

"So, does this mean the two of you are still legally married?" Agnes asked.

"No. Earlier this summer I hired a divorce attorney who could help me expedite the process. We're divorced now."

"You were still married all this time... oh man," she whispered.

"Yeah, another huge mistake on my part. I just keep on making one poor decision after another. Hopefully, now, you can see why I'm not so quick to forget our past."

"Clara, believe me. I'm not looking to gain anything other than a temporary place to lay my head until I get a job. Then, I'm out of here. No strings attached and no hidden agendas. I promise," Agnes responded.

Clara relaxed her posture and began petting Holly, who was now sitting at her feet.

"Ugh, Agnes, what am I going to do with you?" she asked.

Agnes shrugged her shoulders.

"Perhaps give me another chance at being your sister? I may not be perfect, but it can only get better from here," she replied.

"Are you sure about that?" Clara asked.

"I'm positive. I want a fresh start in life across the board. I want to put family first, get a new job, and find myself... I feel like I don't even know who I am anymore," Agnes replied.

"How do you plan on finding yourself?"

"Well, for starters, I'm going to put off dating for at least a year or more if I have to. I've always fallen head over heels, never really taking time to be on my own and discover who I am and what I want out of life. I'm sick of putting men first. This time I really got burned, bad."

"Hmm, I could've told you that was going to happen with Keith. Were you really in love with him?"

Agnes held her head down in shame.

"Yes," she whispered.

"How could you look a man in the eye knowing he's the same man your sister was with? Yuck, just thinking about it makes me sick," Clara said, reverting to the same level of frustration she'd started off with.

"I don't know how to explain it other than you and I were so disconnected for so long... plus, I was trying to fill an empty void, and he showed up just in the nick of time."

Clara got up from her chair, inviting Agnes to follow her for a walk along the shore.

"I can't stand here pretending like I understand... nor do I find any of this to be acceptable. No matter how many times you explain it... it's simply not okay. However, for the sake of not continuously beating a dead horse, I have nothing more to say about you and Keith. Whatever happens is between the two of you. I will not let it ruin my life. Just make sure he doesn't come anywhere near my house or Solomons Island. He's not welcome. Have I made myself clear?" Clara explained.

"Yes, of course. You should know that I feel the same way. It's over for good. Once I tell him about the test results, I have no intention of contacting him anymore. I swear."

"Well, good. As for us... I had every intention of seeing that my locks were changed by the end of the week."

Clara stopped and looked her sister in the eyes.

"But, if you're serious about getting your life together... and I mean serious, then you can stay a little while longer. I, too, had to work very hard to put the pieces of my life together, and trust me... it wasn't easy. We can take this one month at a time, but you'll have to get a job and pull your own weight. In the meantime, maybe we can get to know each other again... and if we can't... we'll be honest about that, too." She offered.

"That would mean everything to me. Thank you so much, Clara. You won't regret it."

"I sure hope not. You showed up at the height of my relationship with Mike. Things were good between us, but somehow, I've allowed my family affairs to get in the way. I'm open to seeing where things will lead with you and me, but I also really need to take some time and rekindle what I have going with him. When you do it right, you can balance romantic love, life goals, and other things of importance while loving your family... you don't have to choose one over the other. I'm learning that the hard way, and I think you are, too."

"I agree. But, it's never too late. Go get him. I know he'll welcome you with open arms, Clara. You're a beautiful woman with a big heart. If he can't see that, then there's something wrong with him, not you," Agnes responded.

"Thanks. Just do me a favor."

"Anything," Agnes said.

"Keep your hands to yourself. This one is mine," Clara said, giving her a devilish smile.

"Well deserved, and you don't have to worry. Scout's honor," Agnes said, holding her hand up, pledging her loyalty.

"Mm hmm."

Clara wasn't ready to hug and pretend as if everything was all better. Their history as sisters still existed; however, for the first time she felt a small, hardened area of her heart being revived again. That had to count for something.

~

Mackenzie sat on one end of the boat, watching Brody pull out of the dock. He brought miniature sandwiches, grapes, and cookies, and even gave her a blanket just in case the early fall-like temperature made her chilly.

"You did all this for me? Everything is amazing, Brody. Thank you."

"No thanks needed. I asked you out... the least I could do was try to make things special for you," he said.

"You went above and beyond special. Everything is perfect. With the scenic Patuxent River as our backdrop, and this meal prepared for two, what more could a woman ask for?"

"Good. I'm glad you like it. If it's all right with you, the plan is to sail a couple of miles out and then maybe coast a little. That way, we can have time to talk while we grab a bite to eat. I'll have to admit I'm a little rusty with dating," he said, fumbling over his words out of nervousness.

"You're fine, and I love the plan. Everything sounds perfect," she said, trying to be graceful while her hair kept whipping her in the face.

"So, is this what you like to do during your downtime? One would think you'd need a break from boats since it's what you do for work."

"I live for the water and beach life. I'd live either near or on the water twenty-four seven if I could afford to," he said.

"Really?"

"Sure, it's the most peaceful place I know. Maybe the mountains would be my backup location, but even that would be an occasional getaway and not a permanent home for me," he replied.

"I'm sure that's one reason the team at Lighthouse Tours works so well together. You're all tied to the water in one way or another. Your knowledge probably helps enhance the customer experience a great deal," she said.

"I'm certain of it. Everybody has their own unique skill set they bring to the table, which is always nice."

He began slowing down the boat a bit, enjoying that Mackenzie didn't mind leading the conversation. He was nervous but continued to focus on giving her the best experience possible.

"What else do you like to do during your free time?" she asked.

"This may sound rather boring, but when I'm off, I like to kick back, throw a few ribs in the smoker, enjoy something cool to drink, and catch up on my sports. There's not much more to it really," he said.

"Oh, come on, Brody. Surely you like to get out

every once in a while? You know, come to think of it, I can't recall one time where you ever brought a lady friend by the café. Do you ever go on dates or at least hang out with the guys?"

He cut the engine off and allowed the boat to continue to glide while he joined her on the other side of his cooler.

"When I tell you I'm a man of peace and solitude, I mean it. I know it might sound strange, and maybe I should even be embarrassed by it, but I like to wind down at the end of a long day's work... and usually that's it. Most of the guys go home to their wives and girlfriends at night and as for me... I got burned by the last girl I dated, so most of the time I just fly solo. It's okay, though... it doesn't bother me. I'm used to it." He admitted.

"Interesting. So, why did you decide to take a chance on me?" she asked.

He could feel his face turning flush, so he busied himself, reaching in the cooler to offer her a drink.

"To be honest, I didn't even think you would say yes. From the look on your face, I think even you were surprised by your own response." He laughed. She joined in with him.

"I plead the fifth. No harm intended, but you caught me off guard, that's for sure." She smiled.

"But, you still said yes. What were you thinking at that moment?"

She shrugged her shoulders.

"What do I have to lose, maybe? I've always thought you were a nice guy... from what I knew of you. Plus, I felt pretty confident that you wouldn't pull anything crazy on me, given that I've known Mike and Ms. Mae for a long time," she said.

"That's a smart way of looking at it. Even though, I'm not the kind of guy who would do anything disrespectful or play games, even if I didn't know Mike and Ms. Mae. My folks raised me better than that."

He chugged down some of his soda.

"Brody, I don't think I've ever asked you where you're from."

"Annapolis, Maryland. My father still lives there in the house where I grew up in Emerald Cove," he said.

"That's wonderful. Are you two close?"

"Very. He has a boat slip out back and just takes off, sailing whenever he feels like it. He's the reason I love it so much," he said.

"I'll bet... what about your mom?"

"She's no longer with us. She's been gone for almost a decade now... she passed from a sudden heart attack. Even the doctors couldn't make sense of why a healthy woman who exercised all the time and was thriving would live such a brief life. It made little sense."

"I'm sorry."

"It's okay. My sister and I really worried about

dad the first couple of years after losing her. But, thankfully, he was able to come around."

"Are you and your sister close?" she asked.

"Yes, but from a distance. She, my brother-in-law, and my niece and nephew are stationed in Colorado at Peterson Air Force Base. He has at least ten more years to serve before he can think about retiring. What about you? Any siblings or close family members, besides your daughter?"

"Nope. It's just me and Stephanie. She's my pride and joy. She's a straight-A student, the president of the Care Club at school that runs food drives for the local community, and she's very kind-hearted. I'm sure all parents say that about their kids, but it's true," she said proudly.

"I believe it. Especially if she's anything like you. I'd love to hang out with her sometime."

"She'd probably like that. Get ready for her to talk your ears off. She inherited the gift of gab from her mother."

"I welcome the conversation," he said, gazing into her eyes.

"To be honest, I can't believe I didn't work up the courage to ask you out before now. You're absolutely beautiful inside and out, Mackenzie."

She felt a tingling sensation at the pit of her stomach and was surprised that Brody, the quiet mechanic from across the street, could leave such an impression.

"Please... call me Mack." She closed her eyes, holding her head up to bathe in the sun before it shifted behind a cloud.

"Keep your eyes closed and listen to the sound of the water gently rocking the boat. Isn't it peaceful?" he asked.

"Yes. It's heavenly. What I wouldn't give to take some time off work and just relax out here for a week."

"That's not impossible, you know. I can help you make that wish come true if that's what you desire to do." He offered.

She opened her eyes and giggled.

"Don't make promises you can't keep. You never know when I might actually decide to take you up on the offer."

"Hey, all you have to do is say the word. In the meantime, how about a sandwich?" he asked.

"Sure."

"Take your pick. I ordered a variety from the deli since I didn't know what you like. It's nothing fancy, but I figured I'd go with something that was easy to bring on a boat."

She looked over the choices and grabbed a ham sandwich. Mackenzie could easily settle for simple rather than a fancy date with a loser.

"Hey, Brody, do you mind if I ask you a question?"

"Go right ahead, I'm an open book."

"Earlier, you mentioned something about getting burned by the last girl you dated... if I'm not prying too much, what happened?" she asked.

He thought for a moment, trying to find the right words.

"We were living together. I made the decision against my better judgment, but she needed a place to stay temporarily, so I welcomed her into my home. I came home early one day... and well... let's just say she had company over."

"Oh."

"Yeah. It took forever to get the image out of my mind. I don't understand what's wrong with people. Is it really that difficult to be honest about how you feel? If someone doesn't want to continue in a relationship, you're under no obligation to stay. All I want is someone who will level with me and tell the truth," he said.

"Don't get me started. I could tell you stories for days."

"I'd much rather hear stories about you, your hobbies, your life growing up, basically everything there is to know about you."

Mackenzie felt like a young girl with an uncontrollable grin displayed on her face.

"Wow, where do I begin?" she asked.

"Anywhere. You have my undivided attention."

"Let's see, I grew up here in Solomons... been here all my life, except for my time spent away at college in Baltimore. As for hobbies, I love to go antiquing whenever I have the spare time."

"Antiquing?" he asked.

"Yes, shopping for antiques. It's really fun." She chuckled.

"Oh, okay."

"Of course, my favorite activity is laying out on the beach, but lately I haven't had the time."

"You know what I hear when I listen to you speak?" he asked.

"What?"

"I hear the voice of someone who works really hard and doesn't take enough time for herself."

"Well, aren't you one to talk?" she said, then she flicked a little water from her water bottle, playfully teasing him.

Brody gasped with an enormous smile, feeling surprised by her sense of humor.

"Oh, so you have a naughty side to you. Okay, you picked the wrong guy to mess with. I'm not afraid of a little water."

"Can you swim?" she asked.

"Of course, I can swim. If needed, I could jump in the water right now and make it to shore and back."

Mack observed the distance to shore, and then locked eyes with him, slowly revealing a smirk.

"No way. Please tell me you're not thinking... what I think you're thinking." Brody laughed.

"Why not? What's a little swim on a first date? Since you want to suggest that I work too much and don't make time for fun… let's have a little fun. Last one in the water is a rotten egg."

"Wait. You want me to jump in the water fully dressed? I didn't bring any spare clothing and neither did you," he said, partially smiling, intrigued, and partially nervous.

"Oh, I think we have a chicken on board. I guess we'll just play it safe and stay in the boat, then… bock, bock, bock." She teased.

He stood up and began removing articles of clothing down to his boxer shorts. He figured it was okay, since a lot of them looked like real shorts, anyway.

She was so shocked, never once thinking he'd take her up on the idea. He seemed more like a run-of-the-mill and abide by the rules kind of guy. Even she was acting out of character, and her adrenaline was pumping.

"Brody, wait. I was just playing around with you. You don't really have to do this."

"No, no, a dare is a dare. Never underestimate the Brodster. That's what my friends called me back in college. I had a reputation for being a daredevil… and, my dear… you just awakened that side of me. There's no turning back now. I'll meet you in the water," he yelled as he climbed to the edge and dived overboard, head first.

Oh, my word. What have I started? she thought to herself.

"Well, so much for pretty hair and nice clothing for our first date," she said, not removing a thing, but diving in headfirst behind him.

CHAPTER 10

fter the tenth knock on Mike's door, Clara's confidence began dwindling. She questioned if she made the right decision to surprise him instead of calling ahead.

She left, making it as far as the driver's side of her car before hearing the creaking sound of his front door.

"Hello, may I help you?" A woman with brunette hair turned on the porch light and stood comfortably in the doorway as if she belonged there.

"Uh, I'm sorry. I must have the wrong house," she said, looking around.

"Actually, that can't be. This is the right house. My name is Clara, I'm looking for Mike," she said, sounding genuinely confused.

In the background, she could hear Mike using a few choice words.

"Diane, whoever it is, tell them I'll be there in just a minute. The fax machine keeps jamming on me. I'll be right up," he yelled.

"Sure," she said and then returned her attention to Clara.

"Sorry. You know how these high-tech machines can be. They look nice and have a ton of buttons, but when we need it to work, we can't figure the darn things out to save our lives. Why don't you have a seat right here on the front porch? I'm sure he'll be with you in just a second. Can I offer you anything to drink?" Diane asked.

Clara took one look at this woman's long gorgeous hair and toned body in yoga pants, and felt sick.

"Would you like to sit?" she asked, pointing toward the wicker chair.

"No. No, thank you. If Mike's busy, I can always catch up with him at the office."

"Are you sure? It will only take a few more minutes. What was your name again? Clarissa?" she asked.

"It's Clara. Clara Covington." She took a few steps backward and then picked up the tempo, feeling like a fool.

What was I thinking? Why would Mike wait around for me to get matters with my sister in order

when he could have another woman in a heartbeat?
She turned, reaching for her door handle, blocking out the rest of their conversation.

"Clara," Mike's voice shouted.

"Clara, I'm here. I just had to fix the fax. Hold on a second," he said, trying to sprint to catch up with her.

She sat in the car with both hands on the wheel, fighting back the burning sensation in her eyes.

"Clara, where are you going? Did you hear what I said? I was caught up with the stupid fax machine. It was literally jamming an important contract that I was supposed to submit a half an hour ago. Why don't you come inside? I'd love for you to meet my cousin, Diane, and her husband Bruce."

"Your cousin?" she asked.

"Yeah, who did you think it was?"

"I don't know. You've never mentioned anything about having a cousin Diane before. How was I supposed to know?"

"True. Well, I have a cousin named Diane who I haven't spoken to in a while. She and Bruce live not too far away from my parents. They actually moved there to be closer to each other. Anyway, they're in the middle of a road trip and made a pit stop to say hello, before continuing on to Florida."

Clara leaned back on the headrest, feeling foolish, yet again.

"Wait. Did you think?"

"Ah, never mind what I was thinking. I just didn't want to intrude if you had company, that's all. Especially company with long gorgeous hair and the body of a physical trainer." She sniggled.

"Well, she is a fitness coach, but I swear I wouldn't do that to you," he said, reaching through the window and confidently laying the sweetest kiss on her lips to reassure her.

"That feels nice," she whispered.

"There's more where that came from. I'm so glad you came here tonight. I've missed you. I need you, Clara. If you're not comfortable opening up and talking with me just yet, I understand. As long as I know you still want me in your life, that's all that matters to me."

"You seemed so distant when we last spoke. I thought you were angry with me... and, well, I know communication with me hasn't exactly been a walk in the park. I just came over here to say I'm sorry. I can do better... I will do better. You're an important part of my life and I can't shut you out. I understand that now," she said.

Mike opened the door and gently tugged on both of her arms, pulling her out of the car.

"Since we're off the clock, I get to do whatever I want without regard for who's watching, right?"

She giggled, nodding her head yes.

"Good."

In the background, Mike's cousin bellowed his name loud enough for the neighbors to hear.

"Mike, your mother is on video chat. Come on in and bring your lady friend with you. We both want to meet her," she yelled.

Mike chuckled.

"Be right there."

Clara nervously tried to check her reflection in the window, but it was rather hard to see in the dark.

"Man, I wasn't prepared for this. How do I look?"

"Beautiful... sensual... amazing. You have absolutely nothing to worry about. Just walk right in there and be yourself."

"I should probably freshen up my lipstick. We were just kissing," she said.

"Just... be... yourself. My folks are going to love you. Come on."

Inside, Mike's parents were on the big screen in his office. Bruce stepped forward first, reaching his hand out to Clara, and Diane went for a hug.

"Mom... Dad... I should be ashamed of not thinking of this video set up before now... this is wonderful. Thank you, Diane, for setting this up for us."

"It's my pleasure. I hold a lot of my classes in person and online, so I figured why not try it tonight," Diane responded.

"Perfect timing, dear. This way, we can finally meet this wonderful woman that my son can't stop raving about. Is that her standing beside you?" his mother asked.

"Yes, Mom. This is Clara. In her defense, she did not know what she was walking into when she came over, so go easy on her." Mike smiled proudly at Clara.

"Hello, Mr. and Mrs. Sanders. It's so nice to meet you."

"My my my... you belong on the cover of a magazine. It's nice to meet you as well."

"Thank you. I heard you just recently moved to Ft. Lauderdale. Are you all settled in and happy with your new home?"

Clara and Mike's family continued talking for a while. It was a pleasant introduction and hopefully the beginning of a bond that would be long-lasting.

Bruce and Diane left around ten, returning to their hotel to prepare for the remainder of their trip. Now that it was just the two of them, they could sit out back, listening to the crickets and catch up over the events of the evening.

"Unbelievable," Mike commented out loud.

"What's unbelievable?"

"Tonight. It was totally unplanned but very much needed," he said.

"You guys have to be more intentional about

planning trips and getting together more often. Busy or not. You'll have Lighthouse Tours for as long as you want... but your parents... not so much. Take it from me. I miss my parents every single day."

"Yes, I would agree with you there. Time with your loved ones should never be taken for granted. I'm going to do better. Starting with the holidays, as Mom suggested. It doesn't matter if they come here or we head south to Florida. Either way, I'm going to see my folks," he said.

"We?" She smiled.

"Ha, you don't miss a thing, do you?"

"It's part of the reason you hired me. I'm detail-oriented, remember?" She teased.

He kissed her temple.

"You certainly are. What do you say we discuss the details of you staying here with me tonight?"

"You make it difficult for me to resist. However, I should get back to the house tonight," she replied.

"Is it your sister?"

"Yes...sorry. She's fine and all, but I just think it's the right thing to do. I actually wanted to talk about everything with you. It's the reason I came over tonight." She admitted.

"You don't have to, you know."

"But, I want to. I overheard your conversation with Ms. Mae. Specifically, the moment where you were questioning my past."

"Clara, I'm sorry. I was upset things weren't

going according to the way I planned and started questioning things for no good reason," he said.

"You have the right to know everything about me if we're going to be a part of each other's lives."

"Wait... how much did you overhear exactly?" he asked.

"Just the part about you wanting to know about my life in New York."

"Is that it?"

"Yes, even though now you're making me speculate." She teased.

"There's no need. Everything is fine. What did you want to tell me?"

"Bottom line... my sister had a pregnancy scare, as I'm sure she already mentioned to you the night I left the house. Thankfully, she took a test, which turned out negative. If it hadn't, I don't know what I would've done with myself."

"You would've survived and continued on, being the best aunt her child could ever ask for," he replied.

"I'm not so sure. Sleeping with your sister's ex-husband is a pretty low-down and rotten thing to do, Mike."

"Yes, if you two were close all these years, it would've been worse. If she believed you were still married to the man, it would've been horrible times two, but all things considered..." His voice trailed off, and all that could be heard was the sound of the crickets for a few minutes.

139

"Are you okay?" he asked.

"Yes, I'm fine. Deep down inside, I know you're right, but it's going to take a minute for me to reach a place of complete forgiveness with her. Where was she for the last ten years of my life? It's pretty pathetic when you're about to lose your job and get evicted and you have no one to call on. No family at all. That's where I was when Joan died. Yet, when her world falls apart, here she comes... expecting me to bail her out, just like she did when she was younger. Some things never change." She grunted.

Mike invited her to sit on his lap, relaxing her head against his shoulders.

"So, where do you go from here?" he asked.

"I whisper a quiet prayer to my parents, like I always do, asking for their advice... I cry a little... and then give the woman a chance to get back on her feet, find a job, and then find a place of her own."

"What about rebuilding your relationship?"

"If that's supposed to happen... it will in time."

She sat up, looking him in the eyes.

"I just want you to know I have nothing to hide from you about who I am, Mike. Nothing from my past or my present. If you want to go to New York and see where I grew up, we can easily book a flight. But, the only other person in this world who truly knows who I am to my core is sitting right in my basement and her name is Agnes Covington."

"I believe you, and I apologize for ever sowing seeds of doubt between us," he said.

"So, does this mean we're good? No more weird phone calls between us at work and two-week breaks from the Solomons office?"

"That was kind of silly of me, wasn't it?" he asked.

"Well, yeah, now that you mention it. I'd like to think we can work out our differences without taking breaks from seeing each other." Her gentle words of correction were followed by soft kisses. After all, she didn't want to bruise his ego, but he had responded rather childishly.

"If you keep doing that, I won't be able to concentrate on what we're talking about."

"Is that so terrible?" she asked.

"No, but before I lose all cognitive ability, I think we should talk about planning our next date... you know... to make up for the one we missed when your sister arrived."

"Ah, yes. How could I forget? I have just the perfect idea to make it special. It's something I recently saw on television."

"I'm open to whatever makes you happy. Send me the information and I will include it in our plans." He offered.

"Nope. This one is on me. Think of it as my way of making it up to you."

"But-"

"No buts," she said, placing her finger on his lips.

"I'll make a few phone calls and see what I can come up with. It will be so romantic. Trust me."

Clara cupped Mike's cheeks in between her hands and whispered words of endearment. Mike, on the other hand, wondered if he'd ever get back to finding the right opportunity to propose.

CHAPTER 11

"Mae, I have a surprise for you... it's for both of us, really. But, it requires you to pack a light bag and make sure you have enough clothes for at least a day," Jonathan said, standing outside the bathroom door as she washed her face.

"A surprise? You know how I feel about surprises, Jonathan."

Mae turned off the sink and leaned closer to the mirror, checking for the remaining remnants of her facial mask. With a few pats to towel dry her skin, she evenly spread moisturizer, turned off the lights, and joined Jonathan in their bedroom.

"What are you up to? We don't have any birthdays or anniversaries coming up soon. Or, at least, not that I'm aware of," she said.

"Who said there has to be a specific occasion in

order to surprise you? Trust me, I think you're going to like this one."

"Did you purchase something without involving me?" she asked, looking at him suspiciously.

"No, Mae. Although, if I did, I'd hope you would trust my judgment."

"It has less to do with trust and more to do with making decisions together. We are married, you know."

"Yes, yes, I know. All the more reason I should be able to surprise my wife without getting the third degree. Now, pack your overnight bag. We leave first thing in the morning," Jonathan said, attempting to leave the room.

"Jonathan, you'll need to do a little better than that if you want me to go along with this last-minute plan of yours. I had my entire Saturday mapped out, starting with a much-needed haircut. You know how popular Trudy is. It will take at least another week to get a new appointment," she said.

"A whole week? That sounds terrible, Mae." He teased.

"Jonathan, I'm being serious."

"So am I. Your hair looks fine the way it is. I never understand why you women go to such great lengths with the face masks, the hair, and all the products in the first place."

"Jonathan, please. If I didn't take care of myself, you'd notice the difference. Trust me. Now, unless you intend on having a wife with split ends and over-grown toenails, let me handle my business tomorrow and perhaps we can reschedule this surprise for our next weekend off."

Jonathan held Mae by the shoulders, looked her in the eyes, and prayed he could reason with her. She could be stubborn and really dig those heels in when she wanted to.

"I only have two major objectives at this point, so I'm hoping you can work with me on this. The first is to go to bed peacefully with you tonight. I hate it when we disagree right before it's time to go to bed. The second is to somehow get you to pack your bags and leave this house with me, so we can experience something special, planned for two. Now, if that means I have to make a few phone calls and rearrange the start time to later in the afternoon, I'll do it. Just say you'll agree to go with me... please?" He begged.

Mae flopped down on the edge of the bed with an enormous smile on her face, ready to accept defeat.

"Since you put it like that, I guess I can be ready by Saturday afternoon. Could you at least tell me what to pack? Will our adventure require a dress or any fancy attire?" she asked.

Jonathan sat beside her, patting his hand on her leg, chuckling to himself.

"Woman, you sure know how to make a man sweat. Good grief. You don't need to pack anything fancy, unless you want to bring that little number you wore on our wedding night," he said, nestling closely beside her.

"You would like that, wouldn't you?" She teased.

"I won't deny it. Okay, I guess it's settled then. I'm going to head over to the office and make a quick call so we can adjust our arrival time. Can I get you anything from the kitchen on my way back?"

"No, thank you, I'm fine. I'm just going to pull out my overnight bag and figure out something to wear," she said.

"Okay, I'll be right back."

∼

On Saturday, Jonathan led Mae, blindfolded, toward an unknown destination. When they arrived, she could hear the familiar sound of water, seagulls, and felt the movement of other people passing them by.

"Jonathan Middleton, I can't believe you made me wear this thing for over an hour. Do you know what it feels like riding in a car blindfolded for that long?"

"I'm sorry, sweetheart. But, it was the only way I could pull this off without you trying to figure out everything. Here... let me untie it for you. It's bright out, so you'll want to open your eyelids slowly."

He removed the blindfold and stood back, waiting for her reaction.

"What in the world is that?" she asked, staring at the boat before her, then checking her surroundings.

"I can tell we're in Annapolis... at Dock's Marina. But, he normally picks out something more-"

"More what? This is a beautiful boat, don't you think? It's called the Blue Turtle. It's a double-decker, fully loaded with all the amenities needed for a special evening for two. Come on. Follow me," he said.

"It's a little different from what Dock normally plans for us. He picked out a regular yacht for our last dinner cruise," she said, trying to keep up with him.

"Let me guess, you arranged this with Dock to try to persuade me on buying a boat like this one, didn't you?"

Jonathan paused. "Mae, we have a wonderful dinner planned in an hour. All I want to do is set sail, freshen up, and have an amazing time with you."

"And we will, but did you set this up with Dock?"

He turned around and made eye contact with her.

"Yes, my buddy Dock helped me. He's always played a role in arranging our adventures, going back to our days of working for Lighthouse Tours in Annapolis. Now... Darlin, are you going to board this boat with me, or are we going to stand here and carry on about the details?"

Mae's posture relaxed as she kissed Jonathan and then passed him by to board the boat.

"How thoughtful of you, love. When you removed the blindfold, I knew immediately where we were. The city of Annapolis. The place where it all began for us."

Mae admired the plush seating in the main living area.

"You know, we probably should ask Dock if he has a few contacts who are looking to sell. Between him and Brody, we should have plenty of options to look at when we're ready."

Jonathan chuckled.

"Yes, of course. But, in the meantime, look around. Go check out the downstairs and tell me how you like it. Take your time... explore. I'm going to check on a few things and I'll be right back."

She explored the lower deck, noticing plenty of space to store the items she brought for the overnight stay. Mae then opened a narrow door leading to the power room that Jonathan mentioned. There was an abundance of wooden carpentry everywhere, that sort of gave the boat a touch of vintage flare.

"Jonathan, are we setting sail already? I thought surely I'd have a minute to run back to the car and get my sunglasses," she yelled.

"You'll have to use mine, dear. The Blue Turtle is on the loose," he responded from above.

Mae returned upstairs to see Jonathan sitting in the cockpit, steering the boat.

"Wait a minute. Last time, Dock made arrange-

ments for us to have a captain. Where's our captain?"
she asked.

He held his arms open wide and proudly. "You're
looking at him. Welcome aboard the Blue Turtle, my
love. My name is Captain Jonathan Middleton, and
tonight I'm taking you on the most romantic adventure of a lifetime, chartered by yours truly."

Mae was a little surprised, but it wasn't the first
time Jonathan went out of his way to prove to be romantic... so she played along.

"Wow, you sure turned things up a notch since
last time. Are you sure you're feeling up to this? Our
tours don't last nearly as long, and I'd hate for you to
get tired and overdo it," she said.

"Come here. You're so kind to always worry
about me, but this time we won't be sailing overnight.
I figured we could explore Chesapeake Bay a little
and head back before it gets dark. Dock made
arrangements for us to stay at the marina overnight.
Don't worry your pretty little head. I haven't lost all
my marbles," he said.

"Aww, I have to give it to you, Jonathan... you
never cease to amaze me. I've never met a man with
so many tricks up his sleeve. I can't even imagine
what you'll come up with next."

Mae stood behind Jonathan, massaging his shoulders. Something about the wind blowing in her hair
and watching her man lead their adventure felt satis-

fying... even a little enticing as she thought about the romantic evening ahead.

"Mae."

"Yes, baby."

"I want to share something with you," he said.

"Go right ahead."

"I may have told you a little fib to get you out here. I figured if I had done it any other way, you may not have come along for the ride."

Her hands dropped to her side, but a smile remained on her face as she considered what he could say.

"You bought the boat, didn't you?" she asked.

He winced a little.

"Yes, was it obvious?"

"Oh, Jonathan. We just talked about this. We were going to do it together, remember?"

"I know, and I swear I had every intention of following through with our plan. The only mistake I made was calling Dock. As soon as I mentioned something about setting a date to drive up and check out a few boats, he told me about this beauty. Mae, this boat was set to be auctioned off as a part of a three-day estate sale. The price was an absolute steal, I couldn't pass it up. It's been checked out by his best mechanic and received a glowing seal of approval," he said.

"For crying out loud, Jonathan."

"Hear me out. I don't want you to think I didn't

consider your feelings. I made a deal with Dock that I'd buy the boat, but if we took it on a test run and you absolutely hated it, he'd help me sell it. He even thinks we could see a profit from the sale if you truly don't like it," he replied.

"That's a relief. I'm glad somebody has some good sense. This is the most irrational thing you've ever done, Jonathan. What's gotten into you? You should be well beyond the point of having a mid-life crisis."

"Mae, can you honestly say you don't like this boat? Look around. Did you take it all in? There are enough beds for the grandkids to take trips with us. We haven't had them over to see us in a while... imagine the looks on their faces when they see their nana and poppa taking them on a sea adventure."

She swatted at him playfully.

"I'm not falling for it, Middleton. You can use the grandkids all you want, but you still owe me an apology. My input when making decisions in our marriage matters, too, you know."

"You're right. I could've gone about this a different way, but I promise, the final decision is all up to you. I'm prepared to go whichever way you want with this. I swear, Darlin. Please don't be upset with me. I was just trying to save us a buck or two, that's all."

"I'd still appreciate being told what's going on in

real-time, Jonathan. What was the final price tag on this boat, anyway?" she asked.

"The bill of sale is right in that drawer over there. Take a look."

She reached over and pulled the drawer open. After combing through the details, she returned the piece of paper where it came from.

"Well... what do you think? Give it to me honest. I can handle it."

"You're one lucky man, Middleton... one lucky man."

"Why is that?"

"Because I was about to ask you to turn this boat around and head back to the marina," she said.

"And now?"

She looked around the boat one last time, admitting to herself that she could get used to it, although she might have picked something slightly different. Mae couldn't deny the thrill she felt running through her veins at the thought of being owners and having the freedom to sail whenever they wanted.

"We can keep it."

As Jonathan continued steering, he reached out with one arm, grabbing her by the waistline.

"Thank you, my love. Thank you so much. I promise, you won't regret it. We're going to have the time of our lives on this boat. Starting with tonight... we can even map out our first real trip if you want to," he said.

"Slow down, tiger. We can talk it over. I swear the day I brought this idea up, I never realized what I was unleashing."

"Ha, well, you did it. I hope you don't see it as a bad thing."

She wrapped her arms around him from behind, giving him a gentle squeeze.

"No, it's not a bad thing. It's actually the best thing that's ever happened to me."

CHAPTER 12

On Sunday, Mackenzie brought her daughter Stephanie and a friend over to spend the afternoon roasting marshmallows and playing volleyball on the beach. It was a much-needed time for her and Clara to catch up and enjoy the last days of somewhat mild weather before the cold started settling in.

The ladies played beach tunes on Clara's outdoor speakers and caught up on their personal lives.

"So... how did it go with you and Brody?" Clara asked.

"We had a delightful time."

"That's it? You had a delightful time, and then what? Are you going out with him again?"

A devilish grin crossed Mack's face.

"We have another date planned for tomorrow

evening. Nothing crazy. We're just going to grab something from the coffee shop down the street so we can talk," Mackenzie said, trying to sound nonchalant.

"A second date... on a Monday evening... which is typically a work night for you. I don't know, Mack. It sounds like you had more than just a delightful time. Tell me all the details. I need some excitement in my life."

"Let's see. He packed a nice cooler for us and took me sailing. I guess you could say we had a late lunch... you know, not quite dinner but way past lunch," Mack said, intentionally dragging out the fun part to tease Clara.

"Right."

"We talked for a while, basically covering all the *getting to know you topics*. Honestly, I can't believe that I've overlooked him all this time. You know how quiet he can be when he's around everybody. I think the only time he comes out of his shell is when he's talking to Mike."

"Mack. Will you get down to it already? Did you kiss?" she asked.

"On the first date? Heavens no. I deserve more credit than that."

She rotated her marshmallow around and then backed away from the fire pit.

"Why did we decide to roast marshmallows when it's seventy-four degrees out here today?"

"Mackenzie!" Clara yelled.

"All right already... we talked for a while, then jumped overboard and went swimming in the Patuxent."

"Shut up. No way. How did you go from getting to know each other to skinny dipping in the Patuxent River?" Clara asked.

"Will you get your mind out of the gutter?" Mackenzie looked around, checking to make sure Stephanie and her friend were still having a good time.

"Nobody said anything about skinny dipping. Although I might keep that in mind for next time." She chuckled.

"Seriously, I don't know what happened. One minute we were sharing a few stories and the next thing I know, I was daring him to jump in the water. Shockingly, he took the bait. I didn't even know the guy had it in him." She laughed.

"Oh... my. Are we talking about the same guy? Brody would never do such a thing."

"You know how the saying goes, never say never. What was I to do? After he went in, I felt obligated to follow through on my end of the deal. After all, I made fun of him by making clucking sounds at him like he was a chicken."

Clara laughed hysterically.

"That sounds like something you would do. So, did you really jump in with clothes on?" she asked.

"Yep. Brody was smart enough to strip down to his boxer shorts. I, on the other hand, wanted to be more ladylike and wait a while before I removed articles of clothing in front of the man."

"Unbelievable. You know what, I shouldn't be surprised one bit. This has your name written all over it. We will forever know you as the life of the party, Mack. I've always loved that about your personality, and it sounds like he enjoys it, too."

"Why, thank you. Now, enough about me. What's up with you and Agnes? I notice you didn't invite her to come outside with us," Mackenzie said.

"We're taking it one day at a time, which is all I'm capable of at the moment. It's a little awkward trying to pretend like everything is normal between us."

"Girl, sometimes we have to fake it till we make it. You might want to reconsider leaving her behind all the time. You can't keep her in hiding forever, Clara. The woman has to get out and live."

"I know. I'm trying to help her sift through the wanted ads so she can line up a few interviews. The sooner she's on somebody's payroll, the sooner she can start looking for an apartment," Clara said.

"Clara Covington. With all the square footage you have on this property, are you really..."

"Yes, I am. A few degrees of separation never hurts."

Mack surrendered, wondering if Clara just needed more time.

"How do you feel about her staying here on Solomons Island?"

Clara let out a deep breath.

"I'm not sure."

"Who would've ever thought after all these years..." Mackenzie grunted.

"I know, isn't it crazy? Look, I don't want to sound like a mean person who doesn't care. I never stopped loving my sister... and I would like to see her get her life in order. If staying here on Solomons Island is what it will take, then so be it. I'll help in whatever way I can."

"That's my girl. It may be difficult now, but you'll feel better about it in the end." Mackenzie reassured her.

Clara perked up.

"I had a chance to talk to Mike."

"That's wonderful. Did you show up at his door wearing something to make the man stutter? I heard it's a sure-fire way to reconcile your differences."

Clara nudged her best friend in the arm, wishing she'd save her untamed hormones for her next date with Brody.

"You are terrible. I hate to disappoint, but I was wearing regular clothing, and I'm glad because his cousin Diane was there with her husband Bruce. Can you imagine how embarrassing that would've been?" She smiled.

"Extremely embarrassing, but I'm glad you met

his family. As long as Mike has been living in Solomons Island, I don't think I ever recall him bringing family around."

"That's because he hasn't. I think he's been going through major guilt over it. He says his time spent in the military caused him to get used to being on his own, but he really wants to connect with his folks and I commend him for it," Clara replied.

"That's good. I'll bet they were really nice."

"So nice... and so welcoming. His cousin Diane arranged it so we could talk to his parents virtually. Mack, it was the sweetest thing. He looks so much like his dad, and after talking to his mother, I can now see where he gets his tender heart from." She continued.

"All I can say is I better have a front-row seat at your wedding. No if, ands, or buts about it."

"Get out of here. You play too much."

"Clara, you know it's only a matter of time. When you've met the right one, you know it. There's no point in belaboring over it."

"Well, it doesn't matter how long it takes, I promise to give you more than a front-row seat. Now let's go over there and teach these girls how to play a proper game of volleyball. If either of them plans to make the team this winter, we have work to do."

Along the way, Clara stopped Mackenzie.

"Mack, before you leave, would you like to come inside and maybe say hello to Agnes?"

"Absolutely," she said, patting Clara on the back.
* * *

By the end of the day, the girls were worn out, and Mackenzie talked with Agnes and welcomed her to the island.

"Agnes, it was so nice to meet you. You're going to love it here. The people are friendly and it's such a small beach town. No one is really a stranger. Well... except for Brody, the hunk I went on a date with recently, but he's not really a stranger. He's just very shy, so I guess that doesn't count. By the way... did I mention he's already spoken for?"

"Mack!" Clara scolded.

"Sorry. Just kidding around. Well, not really," she whispered, as if Agnes couldn't hear.

"It's okay. I'm not dating for at least a year. Plus, I'll be so busy job hunting I'll barely have time, anyway," Agnes responded.

"Oh, dear. I wish you good luck on that one."

"Do you think it will be tough finding employment around here?" she asked.

"No, not at all. I'm sure there's something for you to do. It's the idea of taking a year off from dating. Get ready for taking a bunch of cold showers... been there, done that. No, thank you!"

"Mom, why did you have to take cold showers?" Stephanie asked innocently.

"And that's my cue, ladies. Stephanie, we'll talk about it later, baby. Grab your things, girls, and say thank you to Clara." Mackenzie was halfway to the front door, waving goodbye to her bestie, while trying to consider ways to get around the topic on the car ride home.

Clara locked the door, laughing over Mackenzie's sense of humor.

"She seems nice," Agnes said.

"She is. Mack's been like a sister-" She paused, not thinking first before she spoke.

"It's okay. I think it's great that you've established a network of people that you can rely on out here."

Clara began clearing the kitchen counter.

"Yeah, except they're more than just a network," she said, holding quotation marks in the air.

"Mack welcomed me into her café, made a place for me every week, and in time became a true best friend. For the longest, the only person I trusted was my boss, Joan... the woman who left me this place... and Mackenzie. That's it. They were the first two people to genuinely take me in and care about me after I moved here from New York. It was a welcomed change after feeling so abandoned by my husband and..." She stopped herself, not wanting to dig in too deep.

"You can say it."

"It won't solve anything. All it will do is cause more strife. I made a promise I'd try to avoid that at all costs," Clara responded.

Agnes sighed.

"What good will it do to keep a wall up? Look, I want to help keep the peace around here. I really do. But, don't you think it would be healthy if we at least tried to talk about it?"

"Fine. But, maybe we should create a few rules of engagement. For example, no daggers allowed. Meaning, we can agree to disagree, but no one is allowed to aim below the belt."

"That's fair." Agnes agreed.

"And... if one of us needs a time out from the conversation-"

"Then we have to respect their wishes, and maybe return to the conversation once both parties are ready?" she said.

"I can agree to that. So, who's going to start first?"

"I will. Based on your comment, you clearly think I abandoned you somehow. Yet, I'm the younger sister, and you're the one who left New York, so I don't really see how that could be possible," Agnes said.

Clara gripped her temples and began counting backward to herself. It was a technique she picked up years before she left Keith to help her deal with stress management.

"I'm trying to think of a way to say this without being too harsh. The last thing I recall, the night of mom and dad's funeral, was you getting into an argument with me over their life insurance policy. When the argument was over, you stormed off, never to reach out to me again. I don't recall receiving a hug...

and I certainly don't recall you saying it's okay, sis, we still have each other. You just argued with me over money and left. Between that and being in a marriage with the most verbally and mentally controlling man I've ever met, I had enough. So, I left. You had my phone number if you really wanted to call, but you didn't, Agnes. From my perspective, you couldn't have your way, so you walked out on what mattered most. Family."

Agnes began sobbing deeply. "That's not what happened. At least not from my perspective. You were always the chosen one, and it was clear that mom and dad felt that way, too. They put you down as the sole beneficiary on everything."

"Yes, entrusting me to take care of the both of us with whatever they had left. Which was very little. You know I would've done right by you, Agnes. I always looked out for you, but there was barely enough to cover their funeral expenses. Mom and dad were not rich, Ag. You would've known all this if you had stuck around."

Agnes sobbed with her face buried in her hands before pulling herself together.

"The night I was asking you for money... it was because I was afraid and thought the only way out of my situation was to end the pregnancy."

"What? Why didn't you say something to me?"

"I was ashamed. It was my skeleton... a secret I preferred keeping to myself. At first, I figured having some financial support would help and that would be the end. But the idea of going through with it tortured me so much until I changed my mind. I was determined to raise my child even though I barely had a plan for taking care of myself-"

"Agnes, you know I would've been there for you. No matter what our differences were... we're sisters," Clara said.

"I know that now." She paused before continuing on.

"Back then, I ended up having a miscarriage. The doctor said it was likely stress-induced by everything going on. Losing mom and dad was horrible. Between that and me scrambling day and night, trying to figure out what to do, I guess my body couldn't take it," she said, patting her eyes dry.

Clara held her hand against her chest. "I had no idea, and I certainly don't understand how you made it through all that on your own."

"Yeah... and, to think we spent all these years avoiding each other based on a misunderstanding. Neither one of us was at fault back then. You were doing your best to try to look out for me, and I didn't understand the depth of what was really going on."

Clara leaned on the kitchen counter and exhaled, feeling the weight of her sister's confession. Whenever she heard about stories like this, she always wondered how families could allow conflict to divide them. Now it was easy to see firsthand.

"Aggy," she said, a name of endearment she hadn't used in decades.

"Yes."

"From my core, I'm sorry for everything you ever went through, and I'm sorry that I didn't make you feel loved. I was supposed to be your safety net when mom and dad passed. I feel like I let you down," she said.

"You don't owe me an apology, Clara. I was hard-headed, way too needy, and only considered myself. I'd like to think that's who I used to be, but clearly some of those traits remain if I could entertain the likes of somebody like Keith."

They remained silent for a moment. Clara considered the question that had been brewing in her spirit for a while now.

"You never found Keith to be a little... controlling?" she asked.

"He tried to be way more than a little controlling. I'm not one to get physical, but I'm quick with the tongue. I told him I would not stick around and tolerate his nonsense. No way, I'm not the one." Agnes hoped Clara wouldn't take it the wrong way. But all Clara could seem to do was blurt out in laughter.

"Good. It sounds like he finally met his match," she said.

"You're darn right. It's probably the reason he felt the need to go out there and find another woman. It's okay, his day will come. And, to think all this time, he'd been in touch with you, and I didn't even know it. What a dog."

"We should trade stories over a bottle of bubbly. Maybe even find something to eat. Are you hungry?" Clara asked.

"A little."

"Good. I'll grab a few things out of the fridge, you can grab the glasses." She smiled.

"Clara."

"Yes."

Agnes stretched her arms open wide, inviting her to a warm hug. Neither one of them could promise they wouldn't have future awkward moments or reach their breaking points. But they were sisters, who still loved each other and were willing to figure it out.

CHAPTER 13

M s. Mae, if you wouldn't mind covering the front desk for a few minutes. Clara and I need to go over some things in my office," Mike said.

"Sure, no problem. It's nice to see you two getting along again," she called out as she peered around the corner, watching them disappear into his office.

Inside, Clara excitedly started sharing everything that was on her mind on the morning drive to work.

"I know we have to catch up on business, but you will not believe what I have planned for this Friday," she said.

"Yes, that's right, our date. I didn't realize you were set on this Friday. Before you go into the details, I'd really like to-"

"Oh, Mike. Please, humor me for two minutes. I

really thought you'd want to hear about our date, and also about how things went with my sister last night." She interrupted.

"I'm sorry," he said, not wanting to take away from her excitement.

He sat on his desk and reached out for her hands.

"Tell me everything. Why don't you start with your sister. Is everything okay?"

"Yes, as a matter of fact. We had another long talk. She shared a few things that I wasn't aware of, which helped me to look at everything through a fresh pair of lenses." She admitted.

"Like what?" he asked. Then he thought better of it, realizing it may not be something she was comfortable sharing.

"Wait. Don't answer that if you don't want to. If it's a sensitive topic, I don't want to pry."

"No, it's okay. You're just as much a part of my world as she is. I've finally been able to make sense of our last conversation before I left New York. Agnes was expecting when our parents died. She kept it to herself, feeling afraid that she wouldn't be able to take care of the baby. She'd even considered options for ending the pregnancy but ended up having a miscarriage." Clara explained.

"Wow. She's really been through it. Both of you have in one way or another."

"Sometimes it feels like my family was destined to walk this earth with a dark cloud hovering over us.

Even when we find a little joy, it doesn't seem to last long. It's almost as if we can count on something else bad waiting for us just around the corner."

"You can't think that way, Clara. Last time I checked, your life turned out pretty good, despite everything you've been through. I firmly believe it's because of a series of choices you made along the way. Those choices changed your life for the better. That coupled with blessings from above.... and blessings from Joan," he said.

"And blessings when I met you." She added.

He planted a sweet kiss on her hand, encouraging her to hopefully see things differently.

"That's exactly why I need you in my life, Mike Sanders. You're like the yin to my yang. We balance each other out." She smiled.

"We sure do. Now, tell me, what did you have in mind for this date? I still can't believe you stole my thunder."

"What do you mean?"

"I was the one who was supposed to be planning the last date before things got all out of hand. I was really pumped about it. But, now we have another issue. I kind of... sort of... made last-minute plans for us. I would've told you about this a lot sooner but-" He turned around and reached on his desk for a white envelope and passed it along to Clara.

"Look inside," he said.

Clara wondered what he had up his sleeve given

that she'd already booked a couple's massage for two. She thought it might be a great way to relax and hit the reset button after all the crazy turn of events.

"Two round-trip tickets to Ft. Lauderdale... for this weekend?" she said, not sounding nearly as excited as he thought she would.

"Surprise. I know it's last minute, but I thought you'd like to come with me to meet my parents in person," he said, holding his arms wide open as if he were expecting a hug.

"That's... sweet. Maybe even a little sudden, given that we already had plans. But, sweet," she said.

"Are the plans set in stone? I figured you barely had time to arrange anything since we just talked about it. I'll admit, visiting with my cousin, and doing the video conference was definitely a motivating factor for me. And, I know it's last minute. But, I thought you'd enjoy flying down for the weekend and spending time with the people who brought me into this world," he said enthusiastically. He felt confident that would win her over.

Clara paced around for a moment, quickly trying to come up with the perfect response under pressure.

Come on, pull it together, Clara. It's just a quick weekend trip to meet his parents. But why do I feel so uncomfortable? I mean, there's Agnes, who will be alone all weekend. No, that's stupid. She can take care of herself. The real question is how are you going to respond when they ask about your parents, your past,

*or what brought you to Maryland? You barely under-
stand it all, and you're definitely not ready to talk
about it with anyone else,* she thought.

"Hello over there. I seemed to have lost you. Did
a cat get your tongue?" He teased while walking up
to her, gently tugging on her arm.

"So, what do you say? Will you join me?"

She continued to stew in her own fears.

"Clara, these tickets weren't cheap, but besides
that, I thought you'd genuinely be thrilled to go. Did I
miss something here?"

She didn't know what to say, so she just went
with the first thing that came to mind.

"Of course, I want to meet your parents someday,
Mike, but talk about poor timing." It was yet again
one of those moments she knew she'd later regret.

"What's the big deal? I figured Agnes could
handle a couple of days by herself. We can even
make sure she's all stocked up with groceries if that's
what you're worried about. It would be like a
weekend date for the two of us. Just a quick change in
pace, and we'll be back before you know it. I talked to
my folks, and they really liked you. They want to get
to know you, Clara. I thought that would be something you'd be pleased to hear."

"I am pleased, Mike... this just caught me off
guard. I set my mind on us going for a couple's massage. I had no idea you were planning a big trip. I
want to go... I just-"

There was a knock at the door. It couldn't have been a more awkward moment.

"Ms. Mae, just another minute and we'll be right out," he yelled.

"Your business partner, Kenny, is here. He says he has a 9 o'clock appointment with you," she responded from the other side of the door.

"Darn it. I forgot all about our appointment. I don't have the documents ready," he murmured to himself.

"Look, I can sense your reluctance. I thought this was a fun and spontaneous idea that would allow you to bond with my folks. Not a big deal. I'm still going. Hold on to your ticket and think about it if you want. It's not like the ticket is refundable," he said.

There were three more knocks at the door to which Mike walked over and immediately responded to.

"Kenny, I'm sorry, man. Come on in. Clara and I were just wrapping things up."

She exited the room, looking his way one last time, before taking a long walk back to her desk.

"Must've been one heck of a meeting you two were having. It's not like Mike to forget about his appointments." Mae teased.

A lump that felt like the size of a golf ball was welling up in Clara's throat.

"Ms. Mae, I have a lot of work to get done if you don't mind," she said, walking past Mae.

Her lack of emotion took Mae back, but she decided not to press the matter.

"Sure, honey. My tour doesn't leave for another hour. I'll be in the back if you need me."

"I'm really questioning if I'm cut out for this whole relationship thing." Clara admitted, sitting on her lunch break at the café with Mackenzie.

"Is it that time of the month?"

"Mack, I'm being serious. It's very possible that my ten-year sabbatical left long-lasting effects. Let's face it, I have communication issues, and I'm way too strong-willed for my own good. That kind of behavior is better suited for a woman who's used to being single, don't you think?"

"I'm still stuck on the part where you admitted to being too strong-willed for your own good." Mack teased.

"Funny. Look, I have to be willing to face the music. Maybe things with Mike and I have just run its course. If so, I couldn't blame him. Perhaps I'm not as ready as I thought I was to be in a serious relationship."

Mackenzie placed her hands together, palm to palm, patiently waiting for Clara to speak her mind. As a woman, she could relate to needing a moment to vent. It was natural and usually the result of some sort of internal battle or simply one's way of freaking out.

"The two of you are perfect together in every way. Unless you're going to tell me something terrible like he's cheating or he broke up with you, which I highly doubt."

"No, of course not, but a major part of being in a relationship is opening up and sharing all of who you are with someone else. I'm used to dealing with all of my problems on my own. I just recently arrived at the place where I'm working really hard to do that with Mike, but now he's sprung this trip on me. He's inviting me to fly down to Ft. Lauderdale this weekend to meet his parents. I'm almost certain they're going to ask questions... a lot of questions so they can get to know me, which means getting to know my past."

Mackenzie took a sip of her soda and placed the cup down firmly, looking at her best friend as if she'd lost her mind.

"Really? Is that all you got?" Mackenzie asked.

"Well, yes."

"So, what I really hear you saying is a) Mike is in love and he's ready to take things to the next level. And, b) you've invited fear and doubt to have a front-row seat in your life, therefore eliminating yourself out of something really special?"

Clara thought about the daytime talk shows she used to watch where therapists analyzed one's behaviors and were spot on with identifying the root of the issue.

"I'm not trying to, but my bio isn't exactly squeaky clean, Mackenzie. I can hear them now *asking me questions like... what brought you to Maryland? What should I say...Oh, that's easy, I was actually trying to run away from my ex who was a mentally abusive nut job, and my sister who I didn't get along with... and if that doesn't sound crazy enough you won't believe that after ten years of living in Maryland-"*

McKenzie placed her hand over her best friend's, stopping her before she went too far.

"You don't have to tell them your entire life story. In their eyes, if you're the one Mike has chosen to bring home, that's all that matters." She explained.

"But, how do I explain myself when they ask these kinds of questions? Anything other than what I just told you would not be true. My past feels so broken and with Agnes showing up, I feel like I'm being forced to relive so much of it all over again. Mackenzie, I've never told anybody this, but there were times where Keith looked me in the eyes and told me I'd never amount to anything, and I'd never leave him because I was too much of an imbecile to figure out how to make it on my own."

"Good thing you didn't tell me this when he was on the island. I would've knocked the creep into next week had I known," Mack said.

"Please. I probably should've laid across a therapist's couch years ago, but I became great at suppressing my animosity toward him and my sister. All the way until now at least."

"Only you can answer this... do you really think you became good at suppressing your feelings... Or did this whole thing cause you to develop insecurities? It's never too late to go see a therapist. I did after Stephanie's father walked out on us. It was the only way I could cope for myself and for Stephanie. Traveling the world and joining a rock band... how embarrassing is that? I still don't go around telling that story to this day. I figure no one would believe it, anyway." She chuckled.

Clara checked over her shoulder before leaning closer in.

"A rock band?" she asked.

"Yes, can you believe it? Of all the lame excuses. I've never repeated those words to Stephanie. Don't know if I ever will. It's bad enough I had to tell her he was young and not able to stick around to be a father. The idea that he chose a rock band over her would just crush her little soul."

"I'm sorry, Mack."

"No need to be. Hopefully, your takeaway is this... what you've been through is not up for discussion unless you want it to be. Mike will understand. Now, what I'm really curious to know is how did your sister deal with that numskull's abusive tendencies?"

Clara chuckled.

"Great minds think alike. I asked her the same thing. She claims she had a no-nonsense approach that was too much for him to handle. Now that I think of it, she has a smart mouth on her. We used to go at it all the time as young girls growing up." She smiled, shaking her head at the thought of her childhood memories.

"Sisters. You can't live with 'em, and you can't live without them. At least that's what I hear." Mackenzie added.

"Isn't that the truth?" Clara grunted.

Josh slid into the booth, scooting Mackenzie over so he could give them the scoop.

"Sorry to interrupt, ladies, but I figured you'd want to know this."

"Oh boy, I knew it was a bad idea to take my lunch break in house. What's wrong?" Mackenzie asked.

"Nothing is wrong. Just thought you'd be interested in knowing that Ms. Violet over there is broadcasting her matchmaking skills to the entire bridge club. I overheard something that involved your name and Brody's name, so you might want to look into that. You know the woman is sweet as pie but can't keep a secret to save her life."

Clara and Mack broke out in laughter.

"The second update is Mr. Garrison, the owner, just got off the phone. He said he's coming to the café on Friday and wants to meet with you. His voice sounded rather urgent, so whatever it's about, I wouldn't miss it," he said.

"Why didn't you call me so I could talk to him?"

"Because you were on your lunch break. Duh." Josh rolled his eyes and departed as quickly as he appeared.

"I wonder what it's all about?" Clara said.

"Who knows? The man hasn't really stepped foot in the place since he took over. Maybe he's taken a sudden interest in how business is going. I don't know. Now I'll have to sit around wondering about it all week. Great," she mumbled.

"No, you won't. Tonight, you're going on another date with Brody. I'm certain that will help take your mind off things."

Mack giggled.

"I know. I'm trying to contain my excitement. I keep telling myself we're just meeting for coffee. It's no big deal. Yet somehow I can't stop thinking about what I'm going to wear."

"Look at you. It's only date number two, and you're already smitten. I'll bet it was the skinny dipping that did you in." Clara chuckled.

"Oh, hush. I already told you I didn't take my clothes off."

"Yeah, sure. Don't worry. I won't tell. What happens in the Patuxent, stays in the Patuxent," she said, cracking herself up.

Mackenzie playfully rolled her eyes.

"I'm just kidding. I'm sure he'll be happy no matter what you put on. Just go and have a good time and promise me you won't waste one minute thinking about this Friday," Clara said.

"I will. Promise me you'll give Ft. Lauderdale some serious thought?" Mackenzie asked.

"We'll see."

"Ladies first," Brody said, opening the door to the coffee shop for Mackenzie. A hazelnut scent greeted them as they walked inside. It was a quaint little shop with three tables, including seating for two.

"Thank you."

"I probably should've asked if you're a fan of coffee before inviting you here. This was the only place I could think of knowing that you've already had a long day and need to get home to Stephanie soon," he said.

"Are you kidding me? I drink coffee like it's water. It's a terrible habit, but it gets me through the day. I think this was perfect for a Monday evening. Plus, I love their lattes," she said, inhaling the aroma.

"Good evening, Mackenzie and Brody." Sidney grinned, greeting them from behind the counter. He worked the evening shift a few nights a week for extra pocket change while making his way through his last year of high school.

"It's nice to see you, Sidney," Mackenzie said.

Brody waved, then offered Mackenzie the chance to place her order first.

"I think I'll go with a medium latte."

"Make that two lattes, please," Brody added, winking at Sidney in a way that only they seemed to understand.

"Gotcha. Two lattes coming right up. Why don't you go ahead and grab a seat. I'll bring your lattes right over," Sidney said.

"Thanks, buddy." He then turned to McKenzie with a sweet smile.

"After you..."

Brody pulled out her chair like only a gentleman would, assisting her, then making himself comfortable.

"Do you come in here often?" she asked.

"I pop in every now and again. Mainly if I'm heading home after a quick grocery run. It's a nice treat, but nothing beats making your own coffee at home."

"Oh my gosh, I feel the same way. It's like I'm some sort of coffee snob or something." She giggled.

"That makes two of us. But, I still can't discount the coffee shop. It's all about socialization. Don't get me wrong, the coffee is great, but look at the couple behind us, and the teenagers sitting behind them. They all look like they would enjoy themselves whether they had coffee or not." He chuckled.

Sidney arrived at the table with a tray carrying two lattes and a bouquet of red roses in the other hand.

He passed the roses to McKenzie.

"Lattes for the lovely couple and a dozen roses for the lady. The roses are from Brody, just in case you were wondering," he said.

"Oh, Brody. How sweet is this?" she said, leaning closer to the bouquet to inhale.

"I'm glad you like it," he replied, then he thanked Sidney for going along with his little plan.

"No problem, we're used to getting all kinds of requests here at the shop. If you need anything else, I'm right behind the counter."

He gave Brody a thumbs up and disappeared quickly. The biggest reward came from the look on Mackenzie's face. She was still beaming, which gave him a small inkling of hope that he hadn't completely lost his romantic touch.

"I figured I owed you a do-over to make up for the other night," he said.

"Why is that? We had a wonderful time this weekend. Or at least I did."

"I did, too, but in the name of fulfilling a dare, we both walked away soaking wet. You even more so than me."

She laughed. "Brody, I jumped into the water led by my own free will. You didn't force me. Besides that, I had an absolute blast. I kept replaying the diving scene in my mind and laughing. Stephanie probably thought I was losing my mind."

"Well, good. I'm glad then. Not because your daughter thinks you're crazy, but I'm glad that you had fun. I'll have to admit, there was something about the moment that allowed me to loosen up and stop being so nervous. I guess cold water can straighten anybody up," he replied.

"It sure can. I was so thankful for the public rest stop we found so I could at least try to make an attempt to wring my clothes out before going home. Thankfully, Steph was so engrossed in a game with her sitter she didn't notice me tiptoeing in."

"Gee, that's bad. Next time we go out on a boat we'll have to behave ourselves," he said.

"I'm not making any promises."

Mackenzie hadn't missed the words next time. She liked the idea of there being a third date, even though this one was still in progress... next time still had a nice ring to it.

She looked up to the sight of a familiar person wearing a flannel shirt, approaching the table with a woman by his side.

"Mackenzie," Bill said.

Well, look at this, she said in her mind. Outwardly, she straightened up and returned the greeting.

"Hi, Bill. How are you?" she asked, speaking to Bill, while noticing his date. She had to be at least twenty years younger, was in stellar shape, and was standing there popping her gum so loud it made Mackenzie want to pop her in the mouth.

"I'm good. Cindy and I just came in to grab a quick cup of coffee. I saw you sitting here and thought I'd say hello," he said, nodding his head at Brody at the same time.

"Do you two know each other?" Mackenzie asked Brody.

"I've heard Bill's name before, but I don't think we've officially met," he responded.

"In that case, Bill this is Brody. Brody this is-"

Brody jumped up to offer a handshake and help relieve some of the awkwardness.

"Hey, man. How's it going?" he said, extending his hand.

"Hey there, Brody. Nice to meet you."

Bill's lady friend cleared her throat.

"Gee, where's my manners? Cindy, this is Mackenzie. She works at the café down the street. You really should check it out. The food is amazing," he said.

Cindy gave a half-hearted wave and returned to holding Bill by the arm.

"Everyone in Solomons knows about the café,

Bill. Especially everybody who works over at the lumberyard with you, I'm almost certain of it," she said, assuming she was his new girlfriend from work.

"I'm visiting, actually," Cindy said, snuggling up to Bill even closer. She looked as if she wanted everything but coffee.

"I'm on my way up to see my family in Pennsylvania. I thought I'd make a pit stop to check on this handsome fella on the way. It's been a while, hasn't it Billy?" she said, rubbing his belly.

Mackenzie could feel herself making an ugly face and had to sip on her latte to keep from letting it show.

"Hey, Mackenzie, I was thinking about grabbing these lattes and going for a walk on the dock. Would you like to join me?" Brody asked, hoping to bail her out.

"Excellent idea. Maybe Bill and Cindy would like to have our seats."

Dear Lord, thank you. I owe you one, she thought to herself.

"It was nice running into you, Mackenzie." For just a moment Bill gazed into her eyes. It was almost as if he was sorry that he couldn't speak freely.

She wasn't certain why. If she was keeping count correctly, he was now onto lady number two in no time. Seemed like he had plenty going on in his life to help keep him occupied.

The gentlemen briefly shook hands, and

everyone departed before it became any more awkward.

Outside, Brody held the roses for Mackenzie while they walked over to the water.

"Are you okay? I know it can't be easy running into an old boyfriend," he said.

"Uh, I think the title of boyfriend might be an overstatement," she said adamantly.

"I mean... we dated for a while. I'm sure you heard the story like everyone else on the Island. Bill ended up meeting someone new on the job, or at least that's what he told me. I'm glad we parted ways. Clearly, he has an issue with being honest."

"I hate that for you. If you want, I'll go back in there and knock him out for you. I can send him a message that what he did was wrong in the form of a knuckle sandwich if you want me to." Brody pumped his fist and danced around like a boxer to make her laugh.

"Brody, you're too much." She laughed hysterically. "Wait, you were joking, right?"

"Of course. No need to worry. I was raised to be a gentleman. But, if need be, I'd defend you in a heartbeat."

He noticed her shivering a little and offered her his jacket.

"Thank you. It feels kind of nice knowing that someone would stick up for me if needed. I just don't understand why some men do such dumb things to begin with. Just be upfront with a woman... that's all we ever really want," she said.

"He hurt you pretty badly, didn't he?"

Mackenzie leaned on the railing, taking another sip of her latte.

"He hurt my feelings... maybe even bruised my ego a bit. I've always considered myself to be the kind of woman who could spot a liar a mile away. Apparently, he pulled one over on me. We weren't in love or anything, but I liked him and was looking forward to seeing where things would go."

Brody faced the water and continued drinking his latte.

"I'm sorry. I'm probably admitting way too much at this point," she said. *Mackenzie, you really know how to open mouth and insert foot,* she thought to herself.

"You're good. I appreciate the honesty. I'm learning all the things not to do if I ever want to win you over. Not that I would've ever tried any of that to begin with."

She looked at him, wondering what caused him to like her the way he did.

"I do have one more question for you, if you don't mind," he asked.

"Sure."

He waited a moment, taking in the soothing sound of the waves.

"I know we briefly mentioned it, but what really

made you take a chance on me when I asked you out on a date? I think you gave me the kind version when I asked you before, but the look of hesitancy on your face was revealing."

"Ouch. Was it that bad?" she asked.

"Yes."

Again, she noticed his side profile, his hairline, his clean-shaven face, and the cute smile he gave her when he realized she was staring right at him.

"For one, you caught me off guard. I rarely see you, so that moment when I realized you were actually asking me out, and not just there to order a meal, was actually kind of funny."

"Gee, thanks. Make fun of a guy when he's vulnerable." He teased.

"Hey, cut me some slack. You literally went from ordering corn chowder to asking me to go on a date." She laughed.

"But, you still said yes... so... what was going on in your mind?"

She sighed.

"I feel embarrassed to say this, but I almost said no, coming up with all the reasons why it wouldn't be a good idea. Then, at the last minute... I don't know... I thought maybe it would be a pleasant distraction. What did I have to lose? So... I said yes."

"Has it been a good distraction?" he asked.

"I'm here on a second date with you. That has to indicate something good is going on, don't you think?" She smiled, wondering if the thought of kissing had already crossed his mind.

"Yes, it counts, but if at any point you have regrets about saying yes, I don't want you to feel like you have to hide anything from me. I'm a big boy. I can handle it." He finished his coffee and took her empty cup, stacking them together.

"Brody, I have no regrets. I'm right where I want to be."

"In that case, will you join me for a little stroll?" He smiled and extended his arm to her.

"I don't mind if I do."

CHAPTER 14

"Good morning, Jan. What's on the agenda in North Beach today?" Brody asked the front desk assistant, laying his backpack on the front counter.

"The agenda for today is so long I don't know where to begin. Mike's in his office wrapping up with a phone call, then he wants all the staff to gather for updates before the first tour of the day rolls out. You, my dear, have a gazillion shipments sitting right over there to sort through. If there's any chance you can clear those boxes out so our customers don't have to see them, I'd greatly appreciate it," she said, looking over the rim of her glasses.

Jan was rather new to the company, only a couple of months in, but it didn't feel like it. She always wore glasses hanging from a chain, or positioned on top of her head, and she had a knack for running a tight ship to help keep things in order.

"Yes, ma'am. I'll get right on it," Brody said.

"Oh, one more thing," she said, motioning for him to come back.

"I told the new guy to wait for you in the break room. I think you need to show him your morning routine. The poor thing is always hovering around my desk first thing when we come in. If I can't get back to having my morning coffee without him hovering over me, I'm going to lose my mind." She fussed.

"Say no more. I'm on it. Gary is really great at what he does. He just needs a little more time to get acclimated, that's all."

"I understand. Just teach him how to acclimate himself elsewhere, please and thank you in advance." She had a smirk on her face, but he knew she meant business.

"Can you tell if Mike is off the line yet? I need to poke my head in and speak with him really quick."

She looked down at the telephone.

"He's off the line," she replied.

"Thank you, Jan. You're the best." He tipped his cap and walked away even more chipper and upbeat than usual.

Jan watched him as he swung his bag over his shoulder and passed her by.

In the back, he tapped on Mike's door and waited for a reply.

"Come in."

"Hey, buddy. Just wanted to drop by and let you know everything is all squared away with the boats. Last week I was able to complete my maintenance checks without a hitch, and all repairs are up to date."

"Thanks, Brody," he answered, failing to make eye contact and seeming a bit distracted.

"No problem. Oh, and unless you had something pressing for me, Gary and I are going to pick back up with our training. He's been doing a great job. I think you'll be impressed with his work."

"Yup. That's awesome. If you're impressed, I'm impressed."

Brody stood around for another minute, wondering if Mike would even notice he was still there.

"Okay, guess I'll catch you in the conference room. I'm going to get settled in and grab Gary for the meeting. I'll see you in a few."

"Thanks, man. See you soon."

Brody pulled the door shut, feeling convinced that Mike was off today and not behaving like his usual self.

In the conference room, everybody gathered around a large wooden table, fit for a log cabin, yet cozy and inviting enough to go with the shop's rustic decor. Mike cleared his throat and greeted everybody to get their attention.

"It's good to see everyone this morning. I'm going to keep this meeting sweet and to the point, as I know we all have a lot to do. Last night as I was preparing my notes, I realized that some of us haven't been properly introduced yet. Mainly because you all normally work different shifts, also because I travel between two locations, and the North Beach office is still rather new. Regardless, I don't see any of these reasons as an excuse not to know your teammates. On this rare occasion that we're actually all here, I thought it would be nice to introduce everybody.

"To my left, we have Jan, our lovely office assistant. I tried to call her Ms. Jan, giving her the same respect that we do with Ms. Mae in Solomons, but she wouldn't stand for it." He chuckled and gave her a moment to speak.

"Hello everyone. I may be the oldest, but Jan works just fine for me. Should you need anything, don't hesitate to ask. Oh, and whatever rumors you've heard about me having high expectations for keeping order, it's true. You can believe every word of it." She smiled.

The room lit up with agreeable laughter. By now, everyone had already experienced her version of keeping order in some shape or form.

Mike continued around the circle.

"Next to Jan, we have Brody, who's been with me for so long I've practically lost count. He's always been like a right-hand man to me, and he's our head mechanic."

Brody nodded, showing his appreciation for such a nice introduction.

"Next to him we have Gary, who's actually training with Brody, learning the ropes and eventually taking the reins as it pertains to all things related to the boats," he said.

Gary briefly waved his hand and smiled at the group.

"Continuing on, we also have Chris, Nicholas, and JP who run our tours." Each of them raised their hand as their name was called, offering a warm greeting.

"I also gathered each of you here to commend you for a job well done. Since our opening, Lighthouse Tours of North Beach has been even more successful than I originally expected. Our numbers are looking great, and we've been able to secure local businesses who want us to host their staff events... this comes even as the fall is upon us. Myself, Jan, and Clara at the Solomons location will work together to map out even greater plans to come, but in the meantime, I just want to say thank you for doing such a wonderful job," he said.

The team nodded, seemingly pleased about what he shared.

"Finally, I've referenced the Solomons' group several times in passing. However, I think it's time we all had a chance to meet them. The way I see it, we're all one big family. We just work at two separate ends of the county. I can't think of a better way to learn the business and improve upon what we do than by collaborating with our teammates on the island."

Everyone continued to listen with genuine curiosity.

"I've come up with an idea to better support us in getting to know one another. I'll be asking Clara and Jan to clear our calendars this Thursday afternoon for a few hours. This way we can head down to the island... and for an added adventure, we'll be traveling by boat. Don't worry, I'll get you back in time. But, I think it will be a marvelous chance to let you see the store, meet the crew, and we can all head across the street to the neighborhood café, where you can enjoy some of the best lunch in town. Isn't that right, Brody?" he asked.

"It sure is. Their corn chowder is to die for."

Mike continued. "Yes, it is. Hopefully, if all goes according to plan, we can do this a few times a year, next time inviting our Solomons family to come visit with us, of course."

"I think it's a fantastic idea. I'll be sure to call Clara and coordinate everything with her," Jan said.

"Thanks. Also, if you could put in a phone call to Mackenzie at the Corner Café and ask her to set aside a table for us, that would be great. You and Clara can talk that over as well, just to make sure we're all on the same page."

"I'm on it," she responded.

"All right, that concludes our meeting. Get out there and make it a great day, everyone. As always, if you need anything, you know where to find me," Mike said, wrapping up with the team.

Brody passed a checklist along to Gary, asking him to review it and prepare to help unpack the boxes that arrived when he returned. He then caught up with Mike in the hallway.

"Great meeting in there this morning. Quite the difference from what I saw when I stopped by your office."

"Thanks, but what do you mean?"

"Well, you were distracted. Maybe deep in thought. I'm not sure. You just didn't seem like yourself, and I wanted to make sure everything was cool with you," Brody replied.

"Do you have a minute?"

"I have two. Gary should be occupied for a bit. What's up?"

"Follow me," Mike said.

The guys walked down to the nearby pier before Mike looked at him.

"It's Clara, isn't it?" Brody asked.

"Is it that obvious?"

"To me it is because I know you. You may be able

to fool the others, but you're not fooling me. Are you two getting engaged anytime this century or what?" he asked.

"That was the plan. I have the ring all lined up, and I had the best-laid plans, but all that went down the drain. Now, all that's left is my plans for this weekend. If these plans fall through, then honestly, I'm just going to take it as a sign that my timing is off... way off," Mike said.

"What going on this weekend?"

"I purchased tickets for us to fly down and see my parents in Ft. Lauderdale. She had a chance to meet them virtually this week. When they hit it off so well, I realized... I can't think of a better way to kick off this time in our lives than by having her meet the people who mean so much to me. Plus, I knew my parents would be thrilled to see me since it's been a while. To me it sounded like the perfect idea. But, when I surprised Clara with the tickets, she didn't seem all that enthused. I don't know what went wrong, but it definitely felt like I took a sucker punch right in the stomach." Mike confessed.

"Did she tell you no?"

"Not exactly, but she also didn't jump for joy at the idea. Maybe it's because she made plans of her own, I'm not sure. Apart of me wishes this week was over just so I can board the plane and forget about everything else. But, I can't. Therefore, I'm going to keep my head up, put on the staff gathering this

Thursday, and then on Friday I'm out of here. Hopefully, with her by my side, but even if she's not, I need a change in scenery for a few days." He admitted.

"Hey, I understand. Take as many days as you need. You know I have your back."

"Thank you, Brody. I promise when I get back, no distractions. I'm going to pull it together and get back to running things the way I used to. I can't let my emotions get in the way here at work."

"Come on, Mike. Don't think like that. It's not like anyone else noticed. Besides, in my humble opinion, nothing is suffering other than your ego right now and you know it. I know Clara and I'm almost certain if she showed signs of hesitation about going, there's a good reason for it. Especially with everything you told me she's been dealing with," Brody said, laying it on heavy to get his message across.

"Everything will work out just fine. You just have to stay positive and believe." He patted Mike on the back, reassuring him.

"Maybe by this time next year, I'll be attending your wedding and bringing Mackenzie as my significant other." He added, finding it hard to contain his smile.

"What? Get out of here. Brody, are you serious right now? Since when did you and Mack become an item?" He laughed.

Mike playfully knocked him around for not telling him sooner. They were truly like brothers who worked well together professionally and confided in one another about everything.

"Calm down, you didn't miss much. We've only been out twice. It's been nice getting to know her. We'll have to wait and see where it leads." Brody admitted.

"Well, I'll be. It looks like somebody is smitten." Mike teased.

"You're such a troublemaker. I'm heading back inside before Gary starts looking for me. Catch you later, boss."

"See you later, man."

CHAPTER 15

Clara handed pamphlets to the guests returning from Jonathan and Mae's couple's tour. She highlighted information about upcoming tours and asked them to share it with their friends. After the last customer left, she checked in with them to see how everything went.

"So, give me some feedback. Are the couple's tours here to stay? Do you think everyone had a good time?" she asked.

"I think they loved it. I'm more concerned about Jonathan more than anything else. You know he's a fisherman at heart and nothing makes him happier than when he's out there giving his fishing tours," Mae replied.

"She's right, Clara. I'll do whatever it takes to help Mike out, but when you spend most of your career sharing the ins and outs of fishing on Solomons Island, it's kind of difficult listening to a bunch of seniors trying to rekindle their love lives on a midday tour. Good grief," he said jokingly but was still sincere.

"Oh, I know it's a bit of a change for you, but the good news is Mike still has you mostly scheduled for fishing tours. Don't worry, he knows where your true passion lies."

"Speaking of Mike, where is he today? North Beach?" Jonathan asked.

Just then, Tommy pulled up to the dock, concluding his tour for the morning as well.

"Yes, he's at North Beach today, but stick around. In about ten minutes, as soon as Tommy is done unloading, I can tell you about our plans for the staff tomorrow."

"Sounds good. We're going to head inside and get cleaned up for lunch. See you in ten," Mae said.

Clara repeated the process of handing out pamphlets to Tommy's group and returned inside to the storage room, placing all excess supplies on the shelf. A pair of hands grabbed her by the waistline, startling the daylights out of her.

"Michael Sanders, are you trying to give me a heart attack? I thought you were supposed to be at North Beach today?" she said, scolding him.

"I'm here for about an hour, and then I'm heading over to the museum. The owner asked for a last-minute meeting. He says he's interested in doing business with us so I figured I'd sit down with him and hear what he has to say. I was hoping you'd be happy to see me. Things ended so abruptly the other day. It's not exactly how I envisioned things would play out."

"I know, trust me, I'm so happy to see you. I was just about to tell everyone about the luncheon for tomorrow. Maybe you could stick around for a few minutes while I share the news?" she asked.

He quietly closed the door behind them, ensuring their complete privacy. Then, he held Clara close enough that she could hear his heart beating.

"We really have to stop having these encounters in the supply room. One of these days we're going to get busted, and you know it," she said.

"Not if I install a lock on the door."

"You wouldn't dare."

"Okay, maybe not, but a guy can dream, can't he?" Mike said.

"Mike, the other day when you asked me about-"

He cut her off, placing his finger gently over her lips.

"I spent the entire morning replaying the last few days in my mind repeatedly. I don't know what I said or did wrong, but God knows I didn't mean any harm. Right now, I don't want to think about any of it. I just want you, Clara."

"But-"

"No. No buts. Just you."

He placed his lips on hers, testing the waters to see if she would respond. She kissed him in return, wanting nothing more than to forget about the last several weeks and get back to normal.

"I love you," he whispered.

"Mike, I love you, too, with all my heart. You know I do. But I have to explain."

He placed his lips on hers again, and she didn't refuse. Then there was an abrupt knock on the door, causing them both to jump back.

"I hate to interrupt, but all of us are patiently waiting to hear this announcement. We'd like to enjoy our lunch before round two of tours this afternoon. No rush or anything... just thought I'd let you know," Mae yelled from the other side of the door.

"I told you we were going to get busted," Clara whispered, poking him in the chest.

"Technically, nobody walked in. How about you go out there first? I'll follow behind you in a minute."

"Sure, throw me under the bus," she whispered.

"I'll meet you upfront, Mae," Clara yelled, before continuing her whisper argument with Mike.

"Come to think of it, I've never had a boss who is such a bad influence."

"That's because you never had a boss who was in love with you. Now go on, scoot before they think we're in here doing something we have no business doing." He smiled, wanting to pat her on the backside, but thought better of it. He figured he'd save that kind of behavior for when things were official and she took his last name.

Outside, Tommy occupied himself on the computer, and Mae looked really testy given that it was pushing close to her lunch hour. Her temperament usually fluctuated when she was starving and ready to eat.

"Sorry for the hold-up, everyone. Since Mike can't stay long, I thought it would be perfect timing to announce our plans for tomorrow. As a matter of fact... Mike, would you like to do the honors?" she asked, stepping out of his way.

"Yes, sure I will. This morning I shared with the North Beach team two important things. The first is I think you're all amazing at what you do and without you, this company wouldn't be what it is today. So, in case I don't say it often enough, thank you. I truly appreciate you. The second item is I'd like for everyone to clear your calendars for lunch tomorrow. I'll be bringing the North Beach team to Solomons so we can have lunch together at the café. Jan and Clara are working on the arrangements. All you have to do is bring yourselves and be prepared to have a good time. I emphasized to the North Beach crew that we're one extended family, even if we operate out of two business locations. Hopefully, the sentiment will be shared as you welcome them tomorrow, and again as they welcome you in the near future to do something special up north. What do you think?" he asked.

"It sounds like a perfect idea. Besides, I'll never pass up on the opportunity to have a free meal," Jonathan said, patting his stomach.

"That makes two of us," Tommy added.

"Good, I thought you'd be pleased. Who knows, maybe you'll be able to exchange an idea or two while you're at it."

"You got it, boss. Now, unless you have anything else to share, I have a chicken salad in the back with my name on it. Are we good?" Mae asked.

"We're all set. I actually need to head out of here before I'm late," he said, giving Clara a quick smile.

"Drive safe and call me later. Okay?" Clara asked.

"Will do. Love you."

"I love you, too," she replied.

Clara returned to her desk, watching as he pulled off in his jeep, wondering how she'd find the right words to tell him, that although she wanted to meet his parents sometime soon, now wasn't the right time.

Later that evening, before sunset, Jonathan drove Mae to the Cove, a local marina where they parked their new boat. They strolled down the pier over-looking several boats before finally stopping at theirs.

"There she is. The Blue Turtle, looking just as beautiful as ever," he said, proudly admiring their new toy.

"Jonathan, if I didn't know any better, I'd think there's some sort of love affair going on with you and this boat behind my back." She teased.

"There may be."

"Yeah, well, if that's the case, you better get it out of your system now. We can't keep coming to the marina every time you have a new thought that involves the boat, you know."

"Mae, I know. I'm just excited, that's all. Just dream with me for a second. Now that we have the boat, we can start making plans for our first family outing. I know you're excited, too. When we got back, you immediately called Lily and the grandkids to invite them to come and see the boat," he said, wrapping an arm around her shoulder as they strolled closer to his pride and joy.

"Yes, dear, I called them and they were so excited. Lily said she'd love to get down here, but it's likely it won't be before the holidays. We can't exactly plan a family trip during the winter," she said.

"No, but when they're here we can plan for spring break perhaps... or whenever. The point is, this is only the beginning. Now that our first dream has become a reality, the sky is the limit. We can do anything we want to."

Mae couldn't miss his childlike joy... it was heart-warming.

"Okay, I'm all in. When the kids come for the holidays, we'll lay out the blueprint for our first family trip. What else did you have in mind?" she asked.

He scratched his head, deep in thought, and then gazed at her with a slow, emerging smile.

"This is going to sound wild, I know... and I don't want you to panic... it's not written in stone, it's just an idea," he said.

"Jonathan, spit it out already. You know I can't take it when you do that to me."

"Okay, would you ever consider living on the boat... right here in Maryland? You know, just like we talked about when we were shopping online."

"I don't recall that conversation," she said, turning around and walking away.

"Mae... Mae... Mae, will you wait a minute. I said it was just an idea... slow down, will you?" He pleaded with her.

She paused dead in her tracks.

"Jonathan, my love. I'm all for dreaming with you, I really am. But, can you slow down and smell the roses with me for a second? We just got married, and if you recall correctly, it takes time for me to get adjusted to change. Hello... remember I'm the one who darn near had a panic attack over the idea of giving up my old life and getting engaged. I think I've been as adventurous as I'm ready to be for the remainder of this year. Heck, next year, too. For now, can we just enjoy knowing that we have the option to sail whenever we want to? I'm content with our current setup just the way we have it, and more importantly, I'm content with us, just the way we are." She confessed.

"Aww, Mae. So am I, and I don't want you to ever doubt it for one minute. You'll have to forgive me. I suppose I'm like a kid in a candy shop when it comes to our new boat, but it will never take precedence over you."

"Oh, thank heavens. I thought you were about ready to jump off the deep end with this last idea."

They laughed, locking arms in a side-by-side embrace.

The moment served as a good reminder to Jonathan to always keep first things first. In his heart, no matter how many toys he had, Mae would always be the true apple of his eye.

Later that evening, Agnes prepared a meal for Clara and Mike. Her intention was to have everything fixed and disappear downstairs so they could enjoy a candlelit dinner for two. It was her way of expressing gratitude after everything she'd put them through. She served their plates filled with crab imperial, a creamy delectable dish, sure to make their mouth water, and a tossed salad, and a side of french fries, which was one of Clara's favorite comfort foods.

"Clara and Mike... please make yourselves comfortable... have a seat. I whipped together a crab dish for you. It's just a little something incorporating what Maryland is known for... it's seafood...and it's also my way of saying sorry, of course," she said.

"Sorry? Everything looks amazing. What are you sorry for?" Mike asked.

Clara listened as an innocent bystander, much more aware of Agnes' guilt and desire to make things right and even her desire to carry her own weight.

"Mike, thank you. However, I didn't exactly show up at the best time or under the best set of circumstances. You and my sister deserve uninterrupted time together... you deserve your space to be free to do whatever it is you want without me around putting a damper on things. This meal... it isn't much... but it's a start. It's my way of showing you I'm thankful for having a place to stay for a little while, but I'm also working hard to get out of your hair as fast as I can."

"Agnes, you don't have to rush things along just for the sake of getting out of our hair. We appreciate the gesture, but finding a new job takes time. It just makes me feel good to know you don't have to search under pressure. Something I never had when Joan passed away," Clara replied.

"She's right. Hey, if you'd like, I can put a few feelers out there for you. I'm not sure what hours you're looking for, but we might be able to use your help part-time at the Solomons location of Lighthouse Tours."

Clara cleared her throat. She was all for helping Agnes, but working together part-time and living together full-time under the same roof might be a bit much for either of them to handle.

"Thanks, Mike, but in order to pay my own rent and keep up with day-to-day expenses, I think it's best that I stay focused on full-time work," she said.

She positioned the last plate on Clara's placemat and stepped back, taking in the entire spread, feeling pleased that everything was just so.

"Well, my job here is complete. The candles are lit, the meal is served, and when you're done, all I ask is that you leave the dishes right where they are. Go for a walk on the beach or do something romantic. I'll see you two later on."

"You sure you don't want to grab a bite to eat with us? I feel terrible that you slaved over the oven all day and you're not going to have anything," Clara asked, looking at Mike, who was agreeing with her.

Agnes walked over to the counter and picked up a plate covered with foil, utensils, and something to drink. She held it up for them to see.

"Trust me... I have everything covered. Now, enjoy yourselves and have a good night," she said, exiting the kitchen.

Mike looked at Clara and shrugged his shoulders. "I guess she just wants to do something nice for us."

"Yep. We might as well dig in before it gets cold. Bon appétit," she said.

"Yes, bon appétit is right. I'm starving." He took the first bite and let the food melt in his mouth, savoring the delicious taste of the cream sauce.

"Your sister can cook."

"Oh yes, she's always had a knack for throwing together a delicious meal. She's a natural. She should've gone into culinary arts... I can easily see her as the head chef in a restaurant or maybe even opening her own food truck or something like it," Clara said.

"Why don't you plant a few seeds... help nudge her in that direction while she's searching for jobs? I bet she'd value your opinion."

"I hadn't thought about it before now. I'll say something to her and see how she responds. It's been a long while since I offered any sisterly advice. I just want to make sure I tread carefully, not overstepping my boundaries," she replied.

"Understood, but from what I can tell, Agnes appears to be appreciative and maybe even humbled by the situation. Of course, you know her better than me, so you have to do as you're led."

She pierced her fork through her salad, considering everything Mike was saying.

"Speaking of being led... I know we didn't talk in-depth earlier, but I'm curious to know if you've given any thought to coming with me to Florida this Friday?" he asked.

"Hold your horses. We need to talk and we will, but can we start by asking each other about our day first, like we normally do? I can't believe I'm admitting this, but Agnes is right. We need to get back to some sense of normalcy. Wouldn't you agree?"

"Of course. Let's see, what does normal look like for us on a Wednesday evening? We have a delicious meal... check. We have each other... check. And, I have the pleasure of looking at your beautiful face, which is illuminated by the candlelight... that's a double-check for me," he said, nestling his nose up against hers.

A crease formed on her cheek from a partial smile. "Mike, you know what I mean. How was the rest of your day? In particular, how did the meeting go? Do we have a new contract in the works or what?" She pressed, eagerly awaiting his response.

"We're still working through the kinks. The owner has a lot of grand ideas, which has its place, but I had to remind him that Lighthouse Tours caters to a much smaller crowd. People who come to us love the island and the quaint feel. A lot of his ideas seem more suitable for a big city, which clearly we are not."

"No way. Big city ideas wouldn't go over well with our customers. If people want a big city atmosphere, they can go to D.C.," she said.

"That's what I tried to tell him."

"You know how the saying goes... you win some and you lose some. If this one doesn't work out, perhaps the next offer will be a win. Either way, just stay true to what you believe in. You weren't called to be a business owner for nothing."

"Thanks, babe. I love how you're always so positive and encouraging. Since we've been together, there's never been a time where you didn't support me, making me feel like I can do anything."

An inkling of guilt washed over Clara. He may not find her to be as supportive once she revealed her feelings about visiting his parents. She wasn't ready yet. Perhaps it was out of fear, maybe even a lack of self-confidence, assuming his family was way out of her league. All she knew was she wasn't ready to expose her shortcomings. Not now, and maybe not for a while to come.

The only person I should probably meet is a therapist. How can I open up and share who I am with these people if I'm too embarrassed to share my story... or to talk about why I came to Maryland in the first place? Ugh, she thought.

"Hello... earth to Clara... anyone home?" he asked.

"Sorry," she said, quickly straightening up and organizing the table.

"Maybe I can move a few items over to the sink. I know she said not to, but it's the worst when food hardens on the plates. It won't take long." She continued, trying to deflect the conversation.

"Of course. Please thank your sister again for me. I'm not sure if she'd be interested, but you should say something to her about the food truck idea that you mentioned earlier. If she were to set up shop anywhere from here to North Beach, people would come out in droves to eat her food. Especially during lunch hour and after five o'clock."

"That's a fantastic idea. Licensing would probably be a nightmare, but if she really wanted to pursue it, I'm sure she can figure it out. As long as she's nowhere near the café. Mackenzie would have a cow if Agnes took away her lunchtime crowd." She chuckled.

"True. Okay, so maybe she can find another location somewhere on the island, but think about it... she could cater on her off days when she wasn't working on the food truck. Clara, you know how much of a visionary I am. I love everything having to do with entrepreneurship."

"I know you do, love. The real question is, will Agnes like the idea? If so, where will she get the startup capital? She needs to start with a regular job, don't you think?" she asked.

"Yeah, well, all of these points are valid, but you're right... she has to buy into it and like the idea for herself. I get it," he said.

"Now we're talking. I'll mention something and see what she says. In the meantime, I'm going to grab my cardigan. I hear the dock calling my name."

"Do you want to go sit by the boat? The one you never use, if I might add." He chuckled.

"Haha, funny guy. Yes, come... take a walk with me."

Outside, they walked hand in hand, feeling the coolness of the September evening. It didn't matter what time of the year it was. Clara couldn't deny the peace she felt whenever she heard the sound of the tranquil water or whenever her feet sank into the sand.

"Clara."

"Uh, oh. I recognize that sound in your voice," she said.

"I think it's fair of me to ask what's on your mind. It didn't go unnoticed that you quickly changed the subject when I asked you about coming to Florida this Friday. Plus, you seemed distracted. You know I'll do anything for you, but I don't want to go down this road of not openly communicating with one another. If you don't want to meet my folks, just say so."

She tucked her hair out of the way and kept looking forward.

"It's not that I don't want to meet them. I do," she said.

"Does it have to do with Agnes?"

"No. Not really."

"Well, then help me understand. I feel like I'm at a major disadvantage here. If it's not my parents and it's not Agnes, then I'm clueless as to what it could be," he said.

"It's me, Mike. Not your parents... not you. I'm the one who needs time." She knew this would be the perfect time to reveal her insecurities, but she couldn't. She stood there, unable to speak and unable to think clearly.

"Is this your subtle way of breaking up with me?"

"No. No... not at all."

"Okay," he said, fumbling nervously for his pockets.

"I wish there was something I could say to help change your mind... anything. A part of me is so dumbfounded by all this. One minute we're doing great, the next there's a turn of events in your life and ever since, it feels like everything is falling apart. Life doesn't work like this, Clara. You can't just run every time it gets hard. Earlier this year when Joan's niece tried to threaten your safety, I was right here by your side. I didn't run. Then, when your crazy ex showed up, again, I was here. I didn't run and I darn well could've. Now, all I'm asking you to do is show up for me for one lousy weekend... and the only thing I get is... it's not you, it's me. Maybe I was foolish to get all excited about you meeting my folks. I probably got way ahead of myself, envisioning us being a-" He stopped himself, realizing he'd already gone too far, allowing his emotions to get the best of him.

"Never mind," he said.

Clara didn't know what to say.

"I probably should head home. Tomorrow is a big day with the staff luncheon, and I should get a little more work done before I turn in for the night."

"Yeah, you're right. Everyone is so excited... we should be well-rested and ready for the festivities," she responded.

Mike held up his finger as if he had one more point to make, but let it go.

Instead, he said, "I'll see you tomorrow."

He turned about-face, heading back toward the house. She sank her face in her hands, silencing a heart-wrenching cry.

CHAPTER 16

"The crab cakes are absolutely amazing," Tommy said, patting his mouth with a napkin.

"I decided to go with the brisket... I have two words for you, Mackenzie.... mouth... watering." Jan added, giving her the thumbs up.

Mackenzie picked up the next glass to refill, feeling pleased that everyone was enjoying their meal.

"Good, that's what I like to hear. There's more where that came from. Chef Harold has been preparing for your arrival today. He saved his very best for the Lighthouse team," she said, leaning in so the other customers wouldn't hear.

"Thank you, Mack. It warms my heart to have the entire team here today. In my mind, the café is the heart of the Island. I've met so many wonderful people here," Mike said, glancing at Clara who was sitting a few seats away next to Jan. Mike stood up and raised a glass before everyone, gathering their attention.

"Good afternoon everybody."

"Good afternoon," they responded.

"I'm not one for long speeches, but I want to say a few important words to the group and give you an important update. My entire goal for bringing you here today was to create a bond and give us an opportunity for fellowship. So far, I overheard Nicholas, Tommy, JP, and Jonathan trading tour stories with one another, and the ladies have been sharing some of the craziest customer service experiences they've had since they started working for the company. Since Ms. Mae has been here the longest, I think she has you all beat by a long shot." He joked. Everyone responded with a hearty laugh knowing he was right.

"When I look around the table, I see lots of wonderful people with unique skills and talent, but the one thing we share in common is we're all a part of the Lighthouse Tours family. I planned today, so we'd have an opportunity to bond. We are and will always be better together than we are apart. It goes without saying, the better we are together, the better our company will be. As for updates, those of you who've been around longer know the Annapolis team would normally be here as well. However, I want to announce that as of this week, I'm officially the sole owner of the Solomons and North Beach locations. My partner Kenny and I made an agreement that included us buying out his half of the business... and I should add, there's no need to worry. We're still on wonderful terms with one another. The decision was just in the best interest of him and his family."

Mae clapped, causing a genuine outburst of cheer around the table.

"Thanks, everyone. Outside of the ownership change, everything else remains the same. I'm going to work really hard to ensure we do this quarterly, or at a minimum, a couple of times a year. Continue being the great staff you are... and for now, continue to eat, socialize, and be merry. Cheers, everybody." Mike held up his glass.

"Cheers."

After everyone finished their meal, some remained for dessert and others mingled around the table, catching up with one another.

Brody congratulated his boss and then snuck over to the front counter. "Hello, beautiful," he said to Mackenzie, whose face lit up like the Fourth of July.

"Aren't you supposed to be at the luncheon right now?" she asked.

"I'm going back, don't worry. There was no way I could come in here without saying hello and telling you how beautiful you look today."

"Oh, Brody, stop." She smiled.

"I'm serious."

"So am I. I'm wearing an apron, for Pete's sake. There's nothing beautiful about my work uniform," she said.

"We might have to agree to disagree then. I think you're cute. You always look good in anything you put on."

She looked down at the floor, feeling unusually shy.

"I'm not saying it just to butter you up. I think it's obvious that I'm into you. I came over here because I was wondering if you were free to go out again this weekend?" he asked.

"Oh, I'd like to, but this is the first weekend where Stephanie doesn't have anything going on, and I already promised her we'd figure out something to do together. I'd hate to go back on my word and hire a babysitter."

"Would you be open to finding something the three of us can do? October Fest is open this weekend. Maybe we can go pumpkin picking, visit the corn maze, and eat a few candy apples... you know, pretty much all things fall-related." He smiled.

Mackenzie thought about it. She knew Stephanie would enjoy herself, but this would be the first time she was bringing her daughter around a date.

"If it would help put your mind at ease, I hope you know I will be the perfect gentleman in front of Stephanie. I have a niece and nephew of my own, so I know how impressionable young minds can be," he said.

"I appreciate it and don't doubt that you would be a gentleman. Bringing her out with a guy would be a first for me so, how about I talk to her about the idea and see how she reacts? If I know Stephanie, she'll probably be over the moon, but I just want to be certain."

"I completely understand."

Clara walked up to the counter with a grin, admiring their interaction as a couple.

"Well, well, well. I don't know if there's enough room in this place to accommodate the huge smile on your face. I'm happy to see firsthand just how much you two are hitting it off," she said.

"Something tells me this would be the perfect time to head back over and let you two talk," Brody admitted, saying his goodbyes to Mackenzie.

The women watched him walk away, clearing a good distance before Clara tried to get the scoop.

"Sooo... it looks like you two are really hitting it off," she said.

"We're having a nice time, there's no doubt about it. We get along well, we have a lot in common-"

"But? I feel a but coming on," Clara responded.

"Not really, he just asked me out this weekend."

"Yeah, and..."

"On a family-friendly date, that would include Steph," Mack said.

"Ahh, I see. How does that make you feel?"

"Well, he promised to be a gentleman, which I already knew he would, and we're planning to go to October Fest, so that shouldn't be an issue. I'm sure Steph will love it and all..."

"So, what's the hesitation, then?"

"I'm always concerned about Stephanie getting too attached. He's a really nice guy, but what if things don't work out?" Mackenzie asked.

"What if they do? He's not Bill, Mack. This guy wants to meet your daughter. He wants to connect with the most important person in your life. I say give it a chance. Ease into it, of course, but take a leap of faith at the same time. October Fest is a great place to start."

"Yeah?"

"Yes! Absolutely." Clara reassured her.

"Okay, as long as Stephanie is open, then I'm all in."

"Excellent."

Mackenzie set up a couple of placemats at the counter while she continued talking with Clara.

"So, I talked to the owner of the café yesterday. He adjusted our meeting time because of some rescheduling on his end. Turns out the reason he hasn't been conducting his monthly visits is because he's really sick. His brother-in-law is going to be filling in for him until he's able to get his health back in order."

"Did he say what was wrong?" Clara asked.

"No, only that he needed some time, that he was pleased with the way I was managing things, and the numbers were looking good. He also asked for an update regarding the staff, but you know how he is... this place has always been more of a hands-off investment for him more than anything else. I never complained because I appreciate the freedom to run the ship how I see fit. Despite that, I always thought he'd want to be a little more involved. Either way, I never like to hear about anybody getting sick. I wished him a speedy recovery and told him I was looking forward to meeting his brother-in-law, so we'll see how that goes."

"He's pretty lucky to have you as his head manager. You take good care of this place and the customers as if it were your very own," Clara said.

"We almost lost the café before the change in ownership. I'm just grateful, that's all. This place has always been there for me, putting food on the table for me and my girl. I try to remember that always. But, enough about me... are your bags all packed for your trip tomorrow?"

"Not quite," Clara responded, knowing Mack would disapprove.

Mackenzie looked surprised.

"Don't look at me like that. I told him I'm not ready to meet his parents yet."

"You did what? Have you lost your mind? You

might as well have told the guy you're not interested in being with him in a relationship anymore. Is that really the kind of message you're looking to send?"

"Okay, which question do you want me to answer first? Actually, forget it... I change my mind. I'm not answering any of them here. It's not the time or place. Just know that I thought long and hard about my decision. This is all so spur of the moment and unlike the Sanders family. My life story isn't as squeaky clean as theirs," Clara said.

Mackenzie took her friend by the hand and dragged her in the back to the kitchen.

"Hey, Harold. Don't mind us," Mackenzie yelled to the chef.

Clara waved, feeling slightly embarrassed and out of place.

"I'm only going to say this once, so make sure you catch every word of it. No one is perfect, and no one makes perfect decisions. If Mike loves you, then his parents will love you and want the best for both of you. Period. End of story. Stop allowing these false ideas to take up residence in your mind, Clara. All of it is a lie from the pit of-"

"Mackenzie, I get it. Take a deep breath. You're yelling so loud I can see the customers looking this way through the window."

"I don't care who hears me. You've got yourself a good man and you're about to mess things up because of your own…" She stopped herself, not wanting to crush Clara.

"Insecurities? It's okay, you can say it."

Mack took in a deep breath, leaned forward, and held her friend by the shoulders.

"Look. Women like myself pray to find guys like Mike. He's driven, good looking, kind, honest, he adores you, and did I mention how good looking he is?" She laughed.

"Yes, I think good-looking was on your list."

"Okay, just making sure I didn't miss that one. Basically, he checks all the boxes. As your friend, I will not stand here and try to talk you out of this, but I will caution you to consider one thing. Ask yourself one very important question… is it worth it? Whatever reasons you've been coming up with to not go on this trip… is it really worth potentially losing Mike over?"

Clara started to answer but was interrupted by Ms. Mae, who was peeking through the swinging door.

"Surely you two aren't going to stay back here and miss out on all the fun. Somehow, Tommy and the guys managed to attract Violet's friends from the bridge club over to our table. I've never seen old women flock to a bunch of good-looking men so fast. Clara, I'd be careful if I were you. The one with the cane has her eye on Mike," she said, cackling loud at her own sense of humor.

"Good Lord. I thought Josh and Chloe had the bridge table covered. Let me get out there and do some damage control before the Lighthouse Tours' luncheon turns into a geriatric convention," she said, laughing at her own joke.

Mackenzie left Mae and Clara behind, laughing among themselves, and returned to the main dining area.

"Oh goodness, this sure has been a delightful treat. I'm happy to hear about Mike's full ownership and I'm glad he thought up a way to bring us all together. Years ago, when we were all getting started with the company in Annapolis, we used to have similar outings. It's a great way to boost morale among the teams. Don't you think?" Mae asked.

"Yes, it is."

Mae observed Clara's demeanor, which returned to a somewhat somber state. Perhaps lost in her own thoughts.

"Everything okay with you, honey? You don't seem like you're in a festive mood."

"Oh sure, I'm fine. Everything is great," she replied.

As usual, Mae knew something was up but chose not to pry.

"Mm-hmm."

"I am. Really," Clara said, waving dismissively.

"Well, in that case, I don't know about you, but Chef Harold's brownie à la mode is to die for. I think

I may indulge. The taste of that warm brownie topped with vanilla ice cream hits the spot every time."

"You go right ahead and enjoy, Ms. Mae. I'm just going to grab an extra glass of water from Josh and I'll be right over."

Clara looked across the room, waiting for someone to return to the front counter when her eyes locked with Mike's. If looks could convey a message... his would be one of sadness... maybe even hurt... to which Clara didn't know how to respond. She mouthed the words "congratulations" to him and gave him the space needed to spend time with the staff.

"Jonathan, we have to help intervene with Clara and Mike," Mae said, riding in the car on the way home from work.

Jonathan held his hand up, emphasizing adamantly, "No, thank you. Whatever it is you're about to say, I want no part of it. It's challenging enough to keep up with our own relationship, let alone getting involved in somebody else's," he said.

"What's that supposed to mean? Is that your way of trying to say you're unhappy in our relationship?"

"No, Mae. You know exactly what I mean. There are some things in life people have to figure out on their own. We've been around much longer than Mike and Clara and we're still trying to figure out this thing called love. My honest opinion is you need to leave them alone and let them handle it," he responded.

"But, Jonathan, at least hear me out first. Mike was going to propose the night Clara's sister showed up. Literally, the same night, he planned a nice dinner and everything. I haven't said a word because he confided in me... but ever since then, I've yet to see things get back on track for them. Somebody has to step in and intervene. If not, I'm fearful there won't be an engagement at all."

"Mae... listen to me carefully. It's none of our business. Repeat after me... it's not our business."

"Jonathan, please. If Clara would've taken on that attitude right before we got engaged, the outcome may have been very different."

Jonathan held on to the steering wheel, trying to focus his attention on the road and think of a clever way to change her mind. It just wasn't in his nature as a guy to want to get involved.

"Yes, I agree. However, that was us and their situation is different."

"How so?" she asked.

"Well, for one, it sounds like she has a family situation. There's an added layer that you know nothing about."

"I know enough."

Ultimately, he knew his wife was going to do as she pleased. He recognized they were both bull-headed in that way. Sometimes he had to just suck it up and deal with it, other times she had to.

"Well, there you have it, Mae. Listen, I don't want to argue with my wife tonight. Whatever you decide to do is on you. The only thing I have in mind is taking a nice long shower, watching the game, and spending some quality time with you. That's all that matters to me."

"I'm not sure what you mean by quality time, but the only thing I see myself doing tonight is going to sleep. It's been a long day," she said.

"That's all I want. You lying next to me, sleeping and snoring to your heart's content." He chuckled.

Mae completely denied that she ever snored, even though they both knew better.

CHAPTER 17

*I*t was early Friday, before sunrise, and Clara was scrambling around her bedroom, throwing undergarments and articles of clothing into her overnight bag, when Agnes knocked on the door.

"Come in," she yelled.

"Hey, I was downstairs making a cup of coffee when I heard you thumping around up here. Is everything all right?" she asked.

"Yes, everything is fine. Just a last-minute change of plans. I was going to wake you up, or at least leave you a note, but the short version is Mike asked me to fly down to Florida to meet his parents this weekend. Initially, I wasn't sure, but after thinking about it-"

"Clara, that's wonderful. What do you mean think about it? Are you nuts? What time does your flight leave?" she asked.

"Well, that's the other thing... if I floor it all the way from here to BWI airport, which is practically an hour and twenty minutes away, then I might have just about an hour to park the car and make it to the gate. I won't be back until Monday, but I figured you'd be okay until then, right?"

"Absolutely. Do not worry about me one bit. I have a job interview lined up at a restaurant today. I'm really feeling good about it, and the rest of the weekend I can spend searching for more jobs."

Clara stopped in front of the mirror, haphazardly dabbing coverup under her eyes, hoping it would be enough to revive her appearance.

"Which restaurant?"

"The Seafood Shack up route four just north of the island. It doesn't take long to get there, and the owner seemed really nice," she said.

"It's funny you should mention it. Mike and I were just talking about how talented you are in the kitchen. He thought you might do well with a food truck if you were interested in owning your own business."

"I'd love to run a food truck. I just wouldn't know where to begin," Agnes said, resting on her furniture.

"I'm sure Mike would be happy to help from a business perspective. It might be beneficial to talk to a few food truck owners... you know, to get a solid idea about what's involved behind the scenes."

"Yeah, that sounds great."

Clara slipped into her tennis shoes and checked to make sure she had nicer shoes to wear for the weekend.

"Okay, how about we pick up on this conversation when I get back? I'm leaving a credit card right here in case you need some groceries., and if anything pops up, you know how to reach me," she said.

"Clara, don't worry. I'm a big girl... everything will be just fine. Just focus on getting to the airport safely and let me know when you've landed."

"Of course. Oh, and one more thing. I left Ms. Mae's number on the kitchen counter. She works with me at Lighthouse Tours. Can you call her around eight o'clock and give her the precise message that I spelled out in the note? I just want her to know that I'm with Mike and I won't be back until Monday."

"Sure, no problem."

Clara grabbed her bag, said her goodbyes, and flew out of the house to catch her flight.

"Excuse me. Excuse me, please. Coming through. I'm trying not to miss my flight. So sorry, if you wouldn't mind, may I scoot ahead of you? My flight is boarding, and I really don't want to miss it. Thank you."

Clara maneuvered her way through the crowded security lines. After ten minutes of sheer agony, she made her way to the front to be scanned by a security guard.

"Make sure you remove all jewelry, keys, and shoes. Place everything in the tray to your left, please," he said, pointing to the trays near the conveyer belt.

"I did, sir. I think I'm good to go."

"Okay, step right up."

She stepped inside the body scanner, praying the process could be as quick as possible.

Unfortunately, the alarm sounded as soon as she entered.

"This can't be happening," she whispered nervously to herself.

"Ma'am, try removing your belt. The metal could trigger the alarm," he asked, patiently staring at her.

"Oh yes, the buckle. I'm sorry," she said.

"It happens all the time. Step to the center of the scanner again please," he said, directing her to come forward.

This time she stepped in, holding her breath. After a quick scan from the machine and another scan with the security guard's wand, she was clear to step out and wait for her belongings.

Okay, you got this, she thought to herself, checking the clock to see that the plane had already been boarding for ten minutes. To make matters worse, her carry-on bag was being inspected on the big screen by another security guard.

This is it. It's over. I'm going to totally miss the flight, she thought, feeling her anxiety levels reach an all-new high. On a regular day, it was difficult getting through the airport with minimal stress. But given that Mike was on this flight, pure panic was settling in.

"Ma'am, sorry for the holdup. It was the cosmetic bag that slowed things down. The same thing happens to my wife every single time... and that's after I try to warn her." He grinned.

Clara gave him a half-hearted smile, thanking him for her items before searching for her gate.

"Gate A12 to Ft. Lauderdale, boarding." She read on the big board, then took off, dodging through the crowd like she was playing a professional tennis match. Maybe more like a game of hockey.

As she arrived at the gate, the agent was closing the door.

"Wait. Hold the door. I'm on that flight," Clara yelled.

She handed her ticket to the agent while trying to catch her breath.

"They held me up at the security gate. I'm on this flight... here's my ticket."

The agent inspected the ticket and then looked into Clara's eyes.

"Ms. Covington, I'm sorry, but I'm not able to let you on board. Once the gate is closed, it's closed. Airport policy... sorry."

"But, the plane is right there. I can see it right outside the window. What's the big deal with opening the door again?" she asked.

"Again, it's the airport's rules. I'm just doing my job."

"Can I speak to a manager? This is absurd," Clara asked.

A gentleman walked over, trying to console her.

"Good luck with that. I missed my flight earlier and now I'm hanging around on standby. It's absolutely ridiculous what you have to go through after paying so much money for these tickets," he said.

"Standby... that's it... maybe I can try to catch the next flight or the one after that on standby?" Clara asked the agent.

"Ma'am, we only have two more flights heading to Ft. Lauderdale today, and both of them are extremely overbooked. It's not looking good, but if that's how you want to spend your day, be my guest." The agent then looked beyond Clara, waiting to take the next customer in line.

She glanced at the plane one more time, watching it reverse and then taxi out to the main runway.

Feeling numb from disappointment, she walked back to the parking garage, trying to fight back her tears from falling in public.

～

"Good morning, Lighthouse Tours, may I help you?... I'm sorry, Clara won't be in until Monday. Perhaps I can assist," Mae said, looking surprised to see Clara walking through the front door.

"Sure, I'll leave a message on her desk. She'll call you back as soon as possible. Perfect. Thank you." Mae hung up, waiting for an explanation.

"Ms. Mae, before you ask questions, it's already been a very long morning... I mean, very long. Thank you for handling the front desk, but it won't be necessary to continue. I'm here now." She explained.

"That's all you have to say? It's been a long morning? What is it with you and Mike? I'm done tiptoeing around you two. I told Jonathan I would behave myself and stay out of your business, but something is up, and I won't quit asking until I know what it is."

"Aww, Ms. Mae. I wish I had some earth-shattering news. He's off in Florida with his parents, which is where I should've been this weekend if I wasn't being so darn-"

"Obstinate?" Mae interjected.

Clara looked at her.

"Just calling it as I see it. Now, if you would've communicated with me directly, instead of through your sister this morning, you would've known that Mike is not in Florida."

"He isn't?" Clara asked.

"No. The man caught a nasty flat tire when he

was just miles away from the airport. Poor thing was so frustrated he sounded like he was about to blow a gasket right through the telephone line. Funny thing is, he mentioned nothing about you going with him. He was actually curious to know why you hadn't answered the phone, but I just told him you needed the day off."

"Is he all right?"

"He's fine, just frustrated because he missed his flight, that's all. He said he'll be working from home today."

A smile began emerging on Clara's face.

"This has to be a sign," she said out loud to herself.

"Come again?"

"A sign. This has to be a sign... Ms. Mae, is there any chance you can pretend like you didn't see me today? It looks like I need the day off after all," she said.

"It depends. Does this involve you securing a life-long relationship with Mike? One that doesn't give me agita every time you two have a disagreement?" She smiled.

"I hope. That certainly is the end goal... someday."

"Well, in that case, go get your man. I'll hold down the fort until you get back."

"Thank you." She ran over and squeezed Mae, then grabbed her keys and headed out the door.

CHAPTER 18

Mike opened the door wearing jeans, a white tee-shirt, standing barefoot, with an expression of defeat across his face. Clara stepped in and wrapped her arms around his waistline, resting her head on him.

"I'm sorry, Mike."

He squeezed her lovingly, breathing in the smell of her hair.

"What are you apologizing for?"

"I'm sorry about your tire. I'm sorry you missed your flight... I'm even sorry I didn't say yes the first time you asked me to go with you."

He gently lifted her head, cupping her cheeks between his hands.

"I'm the one who sprung this whole thing on you at the last minute. I should've known it was too much and been more sensitive to everything that was going on."

"You're not upset with me?" she asked.

"No. I couldn't be upset with you if I tried. I just got off the phone with my folks and they were completely understanding. I guess I was just so excited to bring you along that my mind couldn't see past anything else. I knew the whole idea was doomed from the moment I ran over a large piece of metal. It was all she wrote from that point."

"Aww, babe. I'm just glad to know you're safe. The news is filled with stories about people who get injured when they pull over to change a tire."

"Thankfully, I had enough room to get out of harm's way. Do you know the entire time I was out there, the only person who kept coming to mind repeatedly was you? I've missed you, Clara. We've literally spent the last day being distant, barely talking to one another... and for what? Was there anything so catastrophic going on that would cause us to act this way? No. Absolutely not. I never want this much time away from you again. When we're distant, it takes the wind out of me. Please, promise me we won't do this again."

"I promise. Mike, this morning when I woke up, I thought I was going to lose you. I panicked, thinking this was it. I thought once you boarded that plane without me, you would return with a changed heart, disappointed in me, and forever scarred. Suddenly, it made all the things I was worried about seem like nothing in comparison. Then, to make things worse, when I showed up at the airport and the gate was already closed, my heart sank into my stomach. It was the worst feeling in the world."

"You went to the airport, looking for me?" he asked.

"No, I went to the airport, ready to board the plane with you. I packed my bags and flew out of the house so fast it could make your head spin. I have my bags in the car and the luggage tickets to prove it."

"No way." He chuckled.

"Yes, believe me, it's true. I'm in love with you, Mike, and I can't believe that I was about to let my stupid insecurities get in the way of meeting the most important people in your life."

He led her to the loveseat in his living room.

"What insecurities? When I look at you, I see nothing but a beautiful work of art physically, mentally, spiritually... you're everything to me."

"Thank you, but I have a broken past. My marriage and parts of my past were unhealthy and did a lot of damage. I didn't realize just how much until I was forced to face Keith and Agnes. The thought of having to share all that with your parents... I just didn't know what they would think of me."

"My parents? They would adore you... they already think highly of you from the moment you met during our video chat," Mike said.

"Yes, but that was a brief introduction. What happens when your mom asks me why I moved to Maryland? Or when your dad says, how long were you married? The truth about my past has to rear its ugly head at some point. I can't avoid it."

"Clara. My parents are the most loving, accepting, humble, and down-to-earth people you will ever meet. Very much like yourself, which is why I fell in love with you. I really wish you would've told me this a lot sooner. I could've put you out of your misery," he said, closing his eyes and kissing the top of her hand.

"Even if they are nice, people get curious, Mike. It's human nature. I would completely understand if they wanted to know more about the woman you could potentially..."

She paused, feeling uncertain about what she was going to say.

"Marry?" he asked.

"Well... yeah. That's exactly what I meant. Mike, you have to understand, when I think back to all the dumb decisions I made with Keith, the turmoil with Agnes, and even everything Agnes and I are still sorting our way through... I can't help but think your background is way cleaner than mine and perhaps you may have done better with a much less complicated kind of woman."

"That couldn't be further from the truth. I'll never play the comparison game with you. My heart doesn't operate that way, and my parents didn't raise me to look down upon others because of our differences. It's just not how we think. My parents will support you and love you, because I support you and love you."

She hopped over to his lap, feeling relieved and lighthearted again.

"Well, that settles it. When can we book the next flight to Ft. Lauderdale?" she asked.

He chuckled. "I'm going to need a minute to recover from losing those non-refundable tickets, but we'll plan something between now and the holidays. I have to say, this is about the craziest day I've experienced in a long time. I got a flat tire, and you actually tried to catch the flight but missed it. Goodness."

"The agent wouldn't budge. She stood there and watched me staring at the plane as it pulled away from the gate. It was awful." Clara admitted.

"Aww, it's okay. Despite everything, we ended up right where we're supposed to be."

"In each other's arms?"

"Exactly." He planted a warm kiss, and she gladly took in all the affection. She was happy again, feeling satisfied that everything between her and Mike was finally getting back on track.

"Clara," he whispered.

"Yes."

"Come with me, I want to take you to the back

and show you something," he said, extending his hand.

She looked at him suspiciously, wondering what he was up to. He continued, holding out his hand.

"You trust me, don't you?"

She followed him to his office, and he reached behind a stack of books on a shelf, pulling out a box.

"Remember the night I planned a romantic date for us... the evening that Agnes showed up?"

"Yes."

"I had a few surprises up my sleeve for the evening. This was one of them," he said.

He took out a necklace with a heart pendant on it. On the front was the date they met engraved in cursive. She recognized it immediately.

"Mike. How beautiful is this?"

He took the necklace out of the box and opened the clasp.

"Not as beautiful as the woman wearing it. I knew it would look good on you."

She smiled.

"Thank you."

"There's more. But I'll get a second shot at planning a romantic date... a do-over if you will. Do you think you'll be free sometime over the next couple of days?" he asked.

"My entire weekend was dedicated to you, so I think my calendar is clear." She laughed.

"Perfect. Let me make a phone call and see if I

can get us on the calendar for this weekend," he said, pecking her softly.

"As long as we're together, that's all that matters to me."

~

"Brody, do you like apple dumplings? Mom and I always get apple dumplings every time we come to October Fest, right, mom?" Stephanie asked.

"That's right, baby. Apple dumplings with cinnamon."

"You know, Stephanie, I'm embarrassed to admit this, but I've never had an apple dumpling in my life." Brody confessed.

Stephanie was quite amused.

"Never?"

"Never. But, I'm willing to try it," he said.

"Allow me to lead the way." She took off on a mission to show Brody what he was missing.

Mackenzie was pleased to see the two getting along so well. She knew today would be more about Stephanie and Brody's connection, but she was okay with that. She thought it was sweet.

"Stephanie is just like you. She knows what she wants and goes right after it," he said.

"Yep, that's my Steph. Most people will tell you she's my mini-me, for sure."

They continued following behind Mackenzie's

daughter as she made a clear path to the apple dumplings.

"Steph has always been a natural leader, but, I'm curious to know what makes you say that about me? Is there something about my personality that stands out in particular?" Mackenzie asked.

"Are you kidding me? I see the way you handle things at the café. You have such a balanced way of running a tight ship while creating an atmosphere where everybody loves to gather. To this day, I have no idea who the owner is, but we all know who the boss is. I think it's an attractive quality if you ask me."

"Really?" She giggled.

"Yes, ma'am. Not everyone could pull it off the way you do."

Stephanie arrived at the booth that sold apple dumplings and pointed Brody toward the menu.

"See, they have so many choices. Some people like to drizzle their dumplings with sauce, but mom and I like it plain," she said.

"Well, how about we order three plain apple dumplings and choose a picnic table where we can sit down and enjoy?"

"Don't forget something to wash it down with," she said.

"Eh em, don't forget your manners, young lady," Mackenzie said.

"Pretty please." She smiled, revealing her cute dimples.

"Three dumplings and three drinks coming right up."

As the girls walked away to find tables, Stephanie leaned in to share her assessment of Brody.

"Mommy, he's really nice," she whispered.

Stephanie reminded Brody of his niece. She reminded him of how nice it was to be around a little person again, something he hadn't enjoyed in a while since his sister moved to Colorado.

"I was thinking you might enjoy a fun game of corn hole once we're done with our dumplings," Brody said.

"I love corn hole. Me and my friend Grace are all-time champions at school."

"In that case, we should make that our next stop," Brody responded.

"That will be the last game before we leave, okay Steph? We've been here for hours. We don't want to go overboard on our first outing and overstay our welcome," Mackenzie said.

"Okay."

"I'm having a good time," he said.

"So am I. You're like Mom's first boyfriend in a really long time. I mean... really long," she whispered across the table.

She hadn't met Bill, which Mackenzie was grateful for. So it wasn't crazy for Stephanie to assume her mother was rusty in the dating department.

"Stephanie, I think Brody gets the idea. Why

don't you keep working on your apple dumpling before it gets cold, honey," Mackenzie replied. She was mortified, but it wasn't the first time her daughter innocently threw her under the bus.

She tried to laugh it off.

"Out of the mouths of babes."

Brody winked at her.

"Maybe we can do something else fun next weekend, Brody?"

"I'll have to leave that up to your mom. I like the idea if she's okay with it," he said.

"Cool."

With a few more bites, Stephanie was done with her dumplings and begging her mother to check out the nearest game until they were finished.

"Stay right within view. As soon as we're done, we'll play a few rounds of corn hole and then we have to go, okay?"

"Okay."

Mackenzie returned her attention to Brody.

"Thanks for being patient. I should've warned you my kid loves to talk and likes to ask plenty of questions."

"I love it. She reminds me of my niece and has quite the sense of humor," he said.

"Yes, she does."

"I take it she never met Bill?"

"No. We never got around to it. We talked about our kids, but then things took an interesting turn in the relationship. I'm glad to be honest. It may have been a little awkward explaining that whole situation," she said.

"I can imagine. I feel honored that you took the chance in bringing her out with me. It's a privilege to meet her... something I won't take for granted."

Mackenzie let out a sigh of relief. Being around Brody was so refreshing to her.

"Did I say something wrong?" he asked.

"Not at all. I just can't help but wonder why we hadn't entertained the idea of dating each other before now. We were always within close proximity. It's so funny how life works," she said, as she checked to make sure Stephanie was all right.

"I always had my eyes on you. I just had to wait for the right time to make a move." He teased.

She laughed.

"Hey, Mack, do you mind me asking you a personal question?"

"Sure. What's on your mind?"

"What was Stephanie's father like?" he asked, taking another bite of his food.

"Stephanie's father... let's see. You sure you want to hear about him?"

"Yeah, as much as you'd like to tell."

"Well, he was a ladies' man when I met him. I knew it right from the start and gave him a hard time because of it. I was very strait-laced with him for months, sending a clear message that I wouldn't tolerate a guy who didn't have his act together. I think it drove him crazy that I wouldn't give him the time of day. I didn't care. I was a one-man kind of gal and I was looking for a one-woman kind of man."

Brody chuckled. "Good for you."

"That's right. It was almost a year before I ever entertained going out for drinks. By then, I'd noticed a change in him. His interest was shifting from that young bachelor behavior to becoming the guy who was ready to settle down and dig his heels into his career. That's when I started spending time with him, getting to know the depths of him, and started getting serious. We fell hard and fast for each other. On the weekends, he'd invite me over to his garage and show me his drums and instruments... it was his hobby or a passion he had outside of work. A passion that grew throughout our time dating all the way until I had Stephanie. I loved him so much I was willing to support him in all his endeavors. But, I should've known something was wrong when he started spending more time in his garage than with us. The short version is his love for music took precedence over his baby and the mother of his child. He sat me down one day and told me about this grand idea he had to travel the world and make money playing music. To this day I rarely share the full story with anybody, it's way too embarrassing to admit. But, that's him in a nutshell. My ex, the world traveling musician."

"Does he ever reach out to you guys?" he asked.

"Not really. He made very little effort when she was born, and now his visits are nonexistent. I was so enraged at first. Now, it's just become a way of life. I see no point in crying over spilled milk."

"I'm speechless. I didn't realize these kinds of stories still existed in our world today."

"Ha, it happens all the time. Maybe not among your friends and family, but deadbeat dads exist everywhere," she said, while still watching Stephanie.

"Look at her. Despite not having her father in her life, I still think she turned out to be an amazing kid. I know I'm biased, of course."

"I'm right there with you. She's being raised by a phenomenal, strong, smart, and beautiful woman. I bet you'd do anything for her... including giving up your life for her if you had to."

"In a heartbeat," Mack confessed.

Brody glanced at Mackenzie, realizing his admiration and attraction for her was growing with each passing moment.

By the end of the day, Stephanie was slumped over in the back seat of Brody's car, sound asleep. He drove down route four, occasionally watching Mackenzie as she hummed along to the music on the radio. She felt carefree with the wind blowing in her hair, occasionally exchanging smiles with Brody.

"So, you 're a fan of country music, I see," Brody said.

"I can listen to just about anything, really. When I was in college, my girlfriends and I used to dance the night away, singing all the words to our favorite songs. It didn't matter if we had dates or not. We always had a good time."

"Really? I wish I could dance. I usually keep my moves within the realm of a two-step, or something safe so as not to hurt myself or anyone else on the dance floor."

"Haha, Brody, that's hilarious. How bad could it be?" She chuckled.

"You don't want to know."

"You know what... you just gave me a perfect idea for our next outing."

"Oh, no. Please. Why did I open my big mouth? You are chartering into very dangerous territory when it comes to me and dancing."

"I promise to take it easy on you. Everybody knows how to at least sway back and forth. I'm sure something is coming up this fall that involves dancing, and if not, maybe we can enjoy our own private party," she said.

"A private party would at least save me tons of embarrassment."

"Don't be silly. You'll be fine."

"Okay, don't say I didn't warn you," he said.

They continued listening to music for another

mile before she worked up the courage to ask something that had been on her mind.

"So, on a scale from one to ten, how did it feel to go on a date with a middle-aged woman and her young daughter? I mean... let's face it. I'm forty-five, single, and I had Stephanie pretty late. I'm sure that has to leave some sort of impression whether good, bad, or indifferent," she said.

"Wow, you just unpacked a lot in that statement. Hopefully, I can help put your mind at ease when I tell you I had an amazing time, and if you'll allow it, I can't wait to do it again."

She smiled.

"And for the record, I'm also forty-five. I could've sworn we needed at least another five years under our belt before they start throwing the whole middle-aged title out there." He teased.

"Hey, either way, I just accept each year graciously as it comes." She chuckled.

He checked the rearview to see that Stephanie was still sleeping and then reached across the console for her hand.

"This entire day, the only thing I could wrap my head around was whether I was being the perfect gentleman for you and Steph. I hope that sheds a brief insight as to how I feel... and since we're being transparent, I have a question for you," he said.

"What's that?"

"I know this is only our third time going out together. The first date being far more adventurous than I planned... but, how do I measure up from your point of view? At the end of the day, I'm a boat mechanic, who's never had kids of his own. I'm almost certain you had high hopes for meeting someone who could overdeliver after your experience with Stephanie's dad. Do you think a guy like me could ever measure up?"

"Without question, Brody. Of course, I think it's smart for us to take our time and continue getting to know one another, but if you want the secret to our hearts... it's kindness and loyalty. There's nothing like having a man in your life who will love you unconditionally and who you can count on. I'm sure you would agree."

He gently squeezed her hand.

"I agree... and you know what else I think?" he asked.

"What?"

"You and me... I think we're going to do pretty well together."

"Time will tell." She smiled.

CHAPTER 19

"Jonathan, this is one of the most romantic dates I've ever been on with you. What a brilliant idea to find a dock and dine restaurant. We're already getting our money's worth, and we haven't even had the boat for a month yet," Mae said, as she tapped her wineglass with his.

"Finally, my wife is coming around. I figured you might enjoy something like this. Apparently, it's very popular. All you have to do is pull right up to the dock and wait to be served," he said.

"It's beautiful, sweetheart. The food looks great… everything is absolutely wonderful."

"I'm glad you like it. You know, Mae. As I think back over the past year, we've accomplished so much. All of us have. We played a major role in helping

Mike grow the company by giving the most amazing tours in all of Solomons Island-"

"That's right. From Annapolis to Solomons, I don't think there's one company out there that offers the tours and personalized service that we do," she said.

"Yes, then there's us... this year we took our best friendship to a whole new level. I gained an amazing wife, one who took a leap of faith, willing to go on adventures with an old chap like me." He chuckled.

"Jonathan, I didn't even know I could be adventurous until I met you. I still have a lot of work to do, but I'm thankful that you're patient with me as I step out and try."

"Always, honey, even if it means giving you a little nudge now and then." He teased.

Jonathan knew how far he could go with Mae, never really wanting to push her way out of her comfort zone.

"So, I guess the real question is, where do we go from here? What goals would you like to set as we look ahead to our future?"

"Jonathan, one would think it's a new year, with the way you sound."

"No, not a new year. We just have so much life ahead of us and all I want to do is make plans to ensure we enjoy every minute instead of delaying everything. Starting with the holidays... I called my sister and confirmed that she's visiting for the Christmas season."

"And, I called Lily. She's already promised that her hubby and the grandkids are driving down from Jersey, no excuses. After the holidays, I'm prepared to map out our first boat trip for next year, just like we talked about."

"Good. That will be one more thing we can check off the list," he said.

"What kind of list are you referring to?"

"A list of things we'd like to accomplish, big and small, it doesn't matter," he responded.

"Jonathan, is this a bucket list?"

"Not necessarily."

"Then what has you on such a tear lately?" she asked.

"For one, I finally have a partner to do life with. That's an excellent motivator if you ask me. I'm also approaching sixty-six soon. If I don't start now checking things off the list, then when?"

"You couldn't be possibly worried about getting old? You usually blame me for worrying about that, not the other way around."

He reached his fork over, stealing a piece of salmon off her plate.

"Worrying is not in my DNA ...Mae. However, I do have plans to show you the world... so we can have the time of our lives together. That way when I finally do get old, they won't be able to say I didn't do it right."

In return, Mae reached over to sample some of his lobster bisque.

"In that case, I say we make a toast," she said, holding up her glass.

"To?"

"To us. May we live, long, happy, healthy, and adventurous lives together, never missing an opportunity or having regrets." She smiled, tapping his glass.

"I like how that sounds. Come a little closer and give me some sugar."

Mae and Jonathan spent the rest of the evening dining, then sailing back to the marina, fully committed to living out the rest of their lives, planning and orchestrating their happily ever after.

Clara climbed out of the jeep, stepping onto the sands of Chesapeake Beach in utter disbelief. She had been dying to know all day what he was planning for their special date, even setting aside her own ideas. Now that they were here, she was confused.

"Mike, I'm all for being romantic, babe, but we have the most scenic views right behind the house on Solomons Island. Did you really drive forty-five minutes just to lie on Chesapeake Beach?

"I beg your pardon? Are you trying to suggest

that I don't know what I'm doing?" He teased her wearing a smirk on his face.

"No. Of course not. I just don't want you to think you had to burn all that gas in order to have a romantic afternoon together. I love being with you no matter where we are." She confessed.

"And I love that about you. But don't worry about it. Today we're here for a specific reason," he said, tugging on her jacket.

"Do you recall the last time you visited Chesapeake Beach?" he asked.

"Um, let's see. It would have to be when I left New York. I planned a road trip to Chesapeake after hearing such wonderful things about the area. If only I knew back, then I would make Maryland my home. I can't even say that it was a real vacation. I was too focused on getting away from my problems."

"Right. I figured that's what you'd say. Well, I brought you here for a do-over."

"What?"

"You heard me. Close your eyes. I have a surprise waiting for you. No peeking."

She immediately looked around, wondering what Mike could be up to. With the excitement of a little child, she squeezed her eyes shut, holding her hands in the praying position.

"Mike, I can't stand the suspense, hurry."

In the background, she could hear the neighing of a horse.

"All right, you can turn around now."

Her hands covered her mouth as she watched a gentleman escorting two horses over to Mike.

"We're going horseback riding? I didn't even know they did this sort of thing out here," she said.

"Yet another reason you needed a do-over."

"Ma'am, have you ever ridden a horse before?" the gentleman asked.

"Yes, I used to ride all the time at a dude ranch where my sister and I went to summer camp. I'm sure it will all come back to me like second nature."

"Very well then. This is your horse. Her name is Lady, and Mr. Sanders, this here is Rocket. Don't be alarmed by his name. He's very obedient and will listen to your commands."

"Thank you. We have the horses for about an hour, correct?"

"Yes, that's right. My assistant and I will be nearby should you need anything, although with the riding skills you showed when you came for a test run, I think everyone is in excellent hands."

"Thank you," Mike said, and then turned to Clara.

"I didn't have anything crazy in mind... perhaps a slow trot along the shore for a little while. What do you say?"

Before he could wait for a response, Mike's horse started moving after he spoke the word trot.

Clara giggled.

"I thought you said he had skills," she said to the gentleman before taking off to catch up.

"Easy, Rocket," Mike said.

The two caught up with one another trotting slowly along the beach. The day couldn't be more perfect. The sound of seagulls and the ebb and flow of the waves was soothing. Even the horses appeared to be relaxed by it.

"How many favors did you have to call in to arrange the horses?" she asked.

"I have no idea what you're talking about," he said, exposing a dimple.

"Mike, no one else is out here on a horse right now except for us."

He laughed.

"Hey, a man never reveals his secrets. Besides, if I did, it would make it difficult for planning our future romantic outings."

"Future... I love the sound of that word as it pertains to us," she said.

"So do I. Hopefully, I scored an A for creativity on this one. I felt like you needed a fresh start. A chance to create new memories here. You can't erase the events that brought you here... but you can create new memories that hopefully outweigh the dark ones."

She smiled.

"You're so thoughtful, Mike, and you're totally right. I don't have to live with my past forever. I can turn over a new leaf... starting here... starting now."

"You need to give yourself a lot more credit, Clara. You started turning over the leaf the moment you packed your bags and left. I'm just asking you to give yourself permission to be happy again, to live freely without worrying about what others will think, and to focus on creating the life you want. Hopefully... a life that will include me," he said.

"Whoa," Clara said, stopping her horse.

Mike stopped with her and waited for a response.

"There's been a lot of uncertainty in my life as of late, but the one thing I know for sure is I want you in my future," she said.

"Good. Let's keep riding." He began trotting again, leaving Clara slightly behind.

Interesting, she thought, feeling intrigued by his somewhat mysterious behavior.

"Do you recall what you did the last time you were here?" he asked.

"I mainly camped out on the beach for hours, allowing my senses to get lost in the surroundings. I swear being out here is like medicine for the soul."

"I can't argue with that. You ever think that almost eleven years later you'd be standing in the same place with a man you could potentially marry?"

This time, Mike stopped his horse. Any plans for stalling until the end of the date didn't seem right anymore. He was ready to carry out his plans.

She contemplated his question while watching him dismount from his horse.

"Clara, I'm not real good at holding out when I have something big to share. Do you remember when I gave you the necklace I said I had another surprise?" he asked.

"Yes."

"Well, I think now is the perfect time to present you with my other gift."

He pulled a box out of his pocket and looked down at it for a moment.

"I've been waiting a while to present this to you right here on this beach. Truthfully, I got so excited about you meeting my parents, I thought I'd switch up the plans and propose in Florida." He chuckled.

Clara laughed with him, realizing he'd probably been through quite an ordeal.

"Now, I realize, none of that matters. I just want to be with you. I firmly believe when you've met the right person, you know it. No matter the time frame or the circumstances... you just know."

Mike reached out to Clara, helping her dismount from her horse. As she turned to face him, her hair flowed in the wind, her nose was pink, and her cheeks were stained with tears.

"If I would've known this was going to be a tear-jerker kind of day, I would've brought more tissues." She teased.

"Ha, well get ready then, cause I'm going in for the grand finale."

He bent down on one knee and opened the box, presenting a beautiful diamond ring.

"Clara Covington... the day you backed into my car was the best day of my life. Unbeknownst to me, that was the day I met my lover and my friend. To be honest, our purpose for coming into each other's lives had nothing to do with work. The job was just a vehicle for us to get to know one another. I knew from the moment I laid eyes on you I was hooked, and that feeling has only grown stronger. I want to build a life with you... one that includes being there for you... even when life gets tough. I'm down on one knee because I hope you feel the same way, too. Will you marry me?"

Clara smiled.

"So, let me get this straight. You want to marry this crazy girl from New York, spending the rest of your life with her, despite the roller coaster ride you've been on ever since you met her?" she said, pointing to herself.

"I'm all in... knee-deep... ready to spend forever with you."

"Well, in that case my answer is yes," she screamed from the top of her lungs.

He placed the ring on her finger, then lifted her up, sealing the deal with several kisses.

"You know what?" he asked, snuggling up close to embrace.

"What?"

"I think we have at least another forty-five minutes left to finish our romantic horseback ride. What do you think about riding off into the sunset with your fiancé?"

"I think that sounds like a wonderful idea."

On the drive home, Clara held out her hand, admiring her new ring.

"You did a good job, I'm impressed," she said.

"Thanks. It looks beautiful on you."

"Everyone at Lighthouse Tours is going to be so surprised," she said.

Mike thought that was hysterical.

"I'm not so sure about that. I can think of at least two people who already know."

"Really? Well, they sure did a good job of not telling me."

"That's the whole idea, my love."

"Haha. Very funny. Do you think your parents will be happy to hear about the engagement?"

"They'll be through the roof and even more motivated than ever for us to get together," he said.

"All the more reason for us to jump on those tickets as soon as possible."

"Agreed."

She held out her hand for Mike to grab hold of.

"I'm really excited about what the future holds, babe. Can't wait to spend forever with you."

"That makes two of us. Love you," he said.

"I love you."

If you'd like to continue following the characters of Solomons Island in book four, check out the "Also by" section!

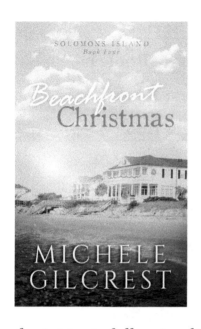

Beachfront Christmas : Solomons Island Book Four

An island filled with the spirit of love and the joy of Christmas!

When Mike and Clara start a new holiday tradition to help save the island, all the characters of Solomons decide to join in. With holiday festivities in full swing, little does Mike know his business, Lighthouse Tours, may need a little help from the town in return.

While beachside festivities are underway, love is in the air which might even spark an unexpected exchange of vows from characters you'd least expect.

If that isn't enough to get you in the holiday spirit, a surprise visitor will show up and offer Mackenzie, the manager at the local café, the surprise of a lifetime. The residents of Solomons and some of her closest friends will be there to show their support, and even share in a little yuletide caroling to celebrate.

Come join Clara, Mike, the employees of Lighthouse Tours, and the locals of Solomons Island for a sweet love story and a beachfront Christmas!

Solomons Island Series:

Beachfront Inheritance: Book 1

Beachfront Promises: Book 2

Beachfront Embrace: Book 3

Beachfront Christmas: Book 4

Also By Michele:

Pelican Beach Series-

The Inn At Pelican Beach: Book 1

Sunsets At Pelican Beach: Book 2

A Pelican Beach Affair: Book 3

Christmas At Pelican Beach: Book 4

Sunrise At Pelican Beach: Book 5